"What a vivid imagination you have, my dear child."

"I never intended to take you in exchange for your brother's freedom. He convinced you that I had designs on your virtue. You offered yourself in your innocence, and I was never a Greek to refuse a gift from the gods. I laid no traps."

Bliss gazed at him incredulously. "But you let me believe that you intended a reprisal unless I married you."

Paris confessed quite shamelessly, and Bliss wrenched off her wedding ring and flung it at him. "I won't stay married to you!" she snapped furiously.

"This time we aren't playing games." His eyes held a deadly glint. "Walk away from me, Bliss, and this time your precious brother *will* be locked up."

Books by Violet Winspear

HARLEQUIN PRESENTS

178—THE SUN TOWER
214—LOVE IN A STRANGER'S ARMS
222—THE PASSIONATE SINNER
226—THE LOVE BATTLE
238—THE LOVED AND THE FEARED
246—THE AWAKENING OF ALICE
288—THE VALDEZ MARRIAGE
300—DESIRE HAS NO MERCY
324—THE SHEIK'S CAPTIVE
354—LOVE IS THE HONEY
420—A GIRL POSSESSED
450—LOVE'S AGONY
492—NO MAN OF HER OWN
566—THE MAN SHE MARRIED
718—BY LOVE BEWITCHED
734—BRIDE'S LACE

HARLEQUIN ROMANCES

1399—BLUE JASMINE
1434—THE CAZALET BRIDE
1472—BELOVED CASTAWAY
1514—THE CASTLE OF THE SEVEN LILACS
1555—RAINTREE VALLEY
1580—BLACK DOUGLAS
1616—THE PAGAN ISLAND
1637—THE SILVER SLAVE
1658—DEAR PURITAN
1680—RAPTURE OF THE DESERT

These books may be available at your local bookseller.

For a list of all titles currently available,
send your name and address to:

Harlequin Reader Service
P.O. Box 52040, Phoenix, AZ 85072-2040
Canadian address: P.O. Box 2800, Postal Station A,
5170 Yonge St., Willowdale, Ont. M2N 5T5

VIOLET WINSPEAR

bride's lace

Harlequin Books

TORONTO • NEW YORK • LONDON
AMSTERDAM • PARIS • SYDNEY • HAMBURG
STOCKHOLM • ATHENS • TOKYO • MILAN

To love is nothing,
To be loved is something,
To love and be loved
Is everything

Greek proverb.

Harlequin Presents first edition October 1984
ISBN 0-373-10734-X

Original hardcover edition published in 1984
by Mills & Boon Limited

CHAPTER ONE

Bliss knew that the Club Cassandra was in Curzon Street in Mayfair, where the shadowy figure of a flower-seller was rumoured to drift through the entrance leaving behind her a lingering scent of the violets in her basket.

As she walked through those same doors Bliss thought of the story which her employer, the clairvoyant Madame Lilian, had stated to be a possibility. She brushed raindrops from her lynx-fur jacket and reflected that on an evening such as this certain environs of London did have a haunted look that played on the imagination.

There was a large Victorian mirror in the foyer of the club and she paused a moment to study herself. Her eyes looked too large for her face . . . she looked anxious and uncertain, and somehow too vulnerable, despite the fur jacket over her long pale dress. Bliss had bought the jacket in a Nearly New boutique and this was the first time she had worn it. She had hoped it would give her a look of assurance, but there was no hiding the fact that she was as tense and nervous as a cat in a strange house.

When she had telephoned for this appointment with Paris Apollonaris he had said he would be at the club at nine; his voice over the line had sounded inflexible and foreign. There had been no need for her to explain why she wished to see him; he had said he had been expecting her to be in touch with him.

The club had stood here in Curzon Street for two centuries, being one of the original gaming houses for the young bucks who would have strolled in with all the assurance of Beau Brummel himself.

In the hands of its present owner it had been embellished to look as it would have looked in Victorian times. There was an atmosphere of mahogany and brass, of plush and ruby port. The staircase which Bliss climbed to the private office of its owner was carpeted in a deep garnet colour, leading to a corridor lit by crystal wall-lights.

As she made her way along the corridor to the door marked Private she could feel the nervous quake in her legs beneath the silky skirt of her dress. It was quiet up here yet with a distant hum of voices from the card rooms, where those rich Arabs would be playing for the kind of stakes which had led Justin into trouble. Bliss couldn't imagine how she was going to persuade the Apollonaris man to be lenient with him, but she was determined to try. She reasoned that he couldn't quite dislike her when two years ago he had proposed marriage to her . . . unless he harboured a grudge against her for refusing his proposal.

She paused in front of the door to his office, bracing herself for this confrontation with him. She hadn't seen him for ages, and it took every bit of her courage to raise her hand and press the doorbell. There was a whirring sound, and when she tried the handle it turned and she entered the room where Paris Apollonaris awaited her.

He was on his feet, standing with his shoulders outlined against the long burgundy curtains that draped the windows, shutting out the rain and the darkness.

Once again his compelling gaze was upon her ... once again Bliss looked into the fierce eyes which seemed never to have known tenderness. There was in those eyes the glint of a keen intellect ... amber eyes like a lion's, Bliss told herself, with lids that slanted downwards so the shadows of his dark lashes fell against his skin.

The line of his nose was utterly straight in the Grecian way. His lips looked as if they had never formed gentle or loving words. Bliss felt his power from across the room and it made her afraid.

'So we meet again, Miss St Cyr.' The grating, iron tones of his voice made her heart sink. 'How long has it been since last we met—two years, if my memory serves me?'

She felt certain his memory never failed him on a single issue that affected his life, and she knew before she spoke that her voice was going to betray her state of nerves.

'I—it must be all of that, Mr Apollonaris.' Her tongue almost tripped over his name and the words scraped huskily from her throat, which felt bone-dry.

'You sound, my child, as if you need a drink.' He approached a drinks cabinet and took from it a long-necked bottle and a pair of stemmed glasses. He had the unexpected grace of movement of tall muscular men, which the smooth cloth of his suit accentuated. He poured the drinks with a hand that was entirely steady, yet Bliss felt certain that anger smouldered in him, banked down and therefore all the more dangerous.

'Come, sit down.' He indicated a leather chair near his desk. 'Take off your jacket and be at ease.'

He was being ironical, of course. He knew very well that she was nervous as a cat; the knowledge was there in his eyes as he watched her approach the chair. She kept on her jacket, for somehow she shrank from having those eyes upon her figure in the pale silk dress. She had been due to dine at Madame Lilian's but had telephoned to say she felt unwell . . . it was only a white lie, for being alone like this with Paris Apollonaris was so unnerving that she actually felt a little faint.

'Your drink.' He placed the wine glass in her hand. 'You are looking quite pale, my child, so the wine should do you good.'

'Th-thank you.' Her voice emerged faintly and she was glad to take a deep swallow of the wine, which had a vintage taste. Paris Apollonaris might have spent his early years living from hand to mouth, but he obviously meant to spend his adult years enjoying the best that money could provide . . . which belied what Justin had said about him, that his enjoyment lay in making the money, not spending it. It was a feeble ray of hope, that money might not be his god.

'That has put spirit into you, eh?' He sat himself down on a corner of his big desk and gazed down at her, and never had Bliss been more aware of body and brain. How did she set about convincing him that Justin was worth his consideration when in all fairness her brother was a swindler who deserved to be punished?

'The wine is very good,' she managed to say, made breathless not by the wine but by his scrutiny ... a sense of mortification swept over her that she had dared to come here so she could ask him to spare the rod that Justin so merited.

'Shall I make it a little easier for you?' Paris Apollonaris leaned forward and pinned her to his gaze. 'You are here at the insistence of your scapegrace brother, is that not so? He hides behind your skirts, eh? He pushes you into the arena with the lion, hoping I shall snap your neck in my jaws while he sits in a bar somewhere, confident that he'll go unpunished as a thief if I find his sister to my taste. Isn't that the way of it?'

'Not quite, Mr Apollonaris.' His gaze seemed to go through her flesh into the marrow of her bones ... the gaze of the fierce Turk in the body of one of those powerful Greeks who had inspired sculptors such as Rodin. A Greek who had worked his way up in the world and wasn't about to write off a stolen sum of money that ran into thousands.

'Then do enlighten me, Miss St Cyr.' A sardonic note had entered his voice. 'I could have sworn your brother was offering you on the brazen arms of Baal, let us say in exchange for his selfish skin.'

Bliss couldn't stop herself from wincing, for that was how it must look, that she had come here to offer herself to Paris Apollonaris in exchange for his promise that Justin wouldn't be prosecuted.

'I—I came to see you,' she said, 'in the hope of making you understand why Justin is the way he is. He hasn't your strength of character, so naturally you find it hard to—to make allowances for his weakness——'

'My child, don't butter me up with references to my strength of character, it's my strength of temper which you need to consider.' He spoke bitingly, letting her know that the courtesy he was showing her was all on the surface and that he was inwardly fuming, as she had guessed.

'I don't blame you for being angry,' her fingers clenched around the stem of her wine glass and she made no demur when he topped up the glass. 'Y-you have every right to be furious, but will it get back your money if you have Justin sent to prison?'

'Hardly.' His eyes glittered. 'But at least I shall have the satisfaction of seeing the little sneak thief behind bars. You don't like to hear him refered to as a thief, do you, Bliss? I see the shadow of pain in your eyes, but he has abused my trust in him, and you surely can't expect me to disregard his crime? I should have to be a soft fool or a saint if I did so, and I'm neither of those things. I'm Greek with a dash of Turk, and I happen to believe in *ekthekissis*.'

She looked enquiring, and after tossing back a mouthful of wine he said succinctly: 'It means vengeful justice, and I'm fully entitled to claim it.'

Bliss drew a shaky breath, feeling not a vestige

of hope that this man would show Justin any mercy. 'My brother's terrified of going to prison—can't you understand what it will do to him to be shut away with hardened criminals? He isn't a criminal in the sense that he plans a crime. He's reckless and the gambling fever is in his blood—if he was really crooked he'd have made a cleverer attempt to cover up his pilfering. You know that!'

'The fact that he is a fool adds to my contempt.' Paris Apollonaris spoke contemptuously. 'Why do you bother with such a brother? Do you imagine he cares for anyone except himself? A dose of prison might cure him of being a selfish and conceited young dolt.'

'Y-you're very hard.' Bliss swallowed painfully. 'Have you no brother or sister that you care about?'

'I am an only child—the son of an unmarried mother.' And as he confided this a brooding look clouded his features, while his eyes scanned Bliss's hair, looped back at her nape in a style that was rather Grecian, perhaps reminding him of the way his mother wore her hair.

'It isn't easy in Greece to be the child of a woman who has no hoop of gold on her marriage finger,' he went on. 'My mother was a goat-girl who minded her flock in the hills where the maquis spread its wild scent. She met a stranger there, he came and he went, and he left her with child. Afraid of the scorn of the villagers, she kept to herself and gave birth to me there in the hills, wrapping me in a goatskin and slinging me across her back when she walked the goats to pasture. I grew up running wild with the flock.'

A brief smile touched his mouth and was gone again. 'I probably thought I was a goat for the first couple of years of my life, and though it was a hard life it was a healthy one. I learned to survive, to take the good weather with the bad, and I grew hardened to the taunts of village children who knew I lacked a father. My mother had striking looks in those days, but she never married; a Greek rarely offers marriage to a woman who has lost her chastity to another man. As I grew into boyhood I became curious about the stranger who had fathered me, but my mother never talked of him. I never learned who he was.'

Paris Apollonaris gestured with his hand in a very Greek way. 'I suspect that my mother never knew his name. They met, they were attracted, they made love beneath the stars ... now thirty-six years later you and I confront each other in the private quarters of a club I own, and in your naïvety—or perhaps your disdain for me—you expect me to say that it's all right for your brother to steal my money—a hell of a lot of *drachmae*! Did he tell you how much?'

Bliss felt the flushing of her skin, mortified by Justin's behaviour and that in pleading his case she must appear to condone his wrongdoing.

'Yes, Justin told me.' The words felt as if they had been wrung from her.

'I used to go barefoot to school, young woman.' The nostrils of the Greek nose were tautly indrawn. 'By the age of seventeen I was driving heavy trucks to the docks, working twenty hours a day, intent on improving my lot. I succeeded, and I never stole a penny piece from anyone!'

Bliss lowered her eyes, an intense feeling of shame sweeping right over her body. Whenever she had heard Justin speak disparagingly of this man she had never reproved him, perhaps because she harboured a grudge against him where Cathlamet was concerned. She hated it that the St Cyr house at York was in his hands . . . she'd never forget with what agony she had wept the day she learned that he had the entitlement to the house in which she had been born. That feeling of bitterness hadn't eased when on the day of her father's burial the family solicitor had read out to Justin and herself a letter which their father had left in his keeping.

In that letter he had explained that it had been upon his insistence that Paris Apollonaris accept the title deeds of Cathlamet, so heavily mortgaged that there had been no way it could stay in the St Cyr family. In exchange for those deeds Bliss's father had borrowed a sum sufficient to finish the education of his son and daughter.

Why, she wondered bleakly, had he not taken them out of their expensive schools and explained to them that their life was going to be less indulged and less privileged because he no longer had the kind of income that permitted them to live in a great house like Cathlamet, with servants to wait upon them, fine horses in the stable, and the expectation of a country life of ease?

Why had he taken away their pride by allowing them to be educated at the expense of a stranger, who now had the right to judge their behaviour ... but at least he couldn't say of her that she didn't earn her own living!

'Is your mother still alive, Mr Apollonaris?' she found herself asking. She had never been curious about his family before; he had always seemed one of those self-made men who sprang from rock rather than flesh.

'Yes, my mother still lives,' he replied in the deep voice with its careful enunciation of English, which he had probably learned from a teacher of languages. His vocabulary was good, his Greek intonation adding a note of significance to his speech. Bliss felt the determination that ruled his life, born to poverty but with a brain that matched his ambitions. His education at a village school would have been basic, except that some trick of birth had given him a clever and acquisitive mind.

'Is your mother living at—at Cathlamet?' Bliss tried not to show her resentment at the very idea of another woman walking through the rooms she had played in as a child, watching the roses grow in the garden walled with Yorkstone, hearing the wind across the moors.

Bliss adored the place, where generations of the St Cyr family had lived, loved and died. It wrenched at her heart to confront this man who had the right to do whatever he wished with Cathlamet; to have living there whoever pleased him.

His lion-coloured eyes looked directly into hers, as if he were reading her thoughts. 'My mother chooses to live in her own country, where

she can feel the hot Greek sun on her skin. She
has no wish to be the mistress of a great stone
house on the moors where the wind is always
blowing.'

Bliss half-closed her eyes, as people do when in
pain.

'You are always welcome to visit Cathlamet.'
Paris Apollonaris spoke without emotion. 'Very
little has been changed there.'

'The house is nothing more to do with me.'
Bliss spoke coldly because she felt cold and could
never be warmed again by those huge log fires
that used to burn in the Yorkstone fireplaces in
wintertime. She caught her breath in loss and
pain and told herself not to think about
Cathlamet. She dragged her thoughts away from
the house whose walls were of the same durable
and creamy stone that made York Minster so
incredibly beautiful.

She looked instead at Paris Apollonaris into
whose skin the Greek sun was baked so that his
golden eyes looked even more distinct and
threatening. How did she persuade such a man to
relent . . .? Even as she asked herself the question
Bliss found an answer that was dreadfully
disturbing. She stared into the slanting eyes of
the Greek who held her brother to ransom and
the frightening thump of her heart confirmed
what she suddenly suspected.

Shrewd about people and money, he had
guessed that Justin would be unable to work at
the Club Cassandra without one day helping
himself to some of the club's revenue . . . he had
known, just as she had, that her brother had no

business working in a place where there was the eternal clink of coin and dice.

'You knew he'd do it, didn't you?' Her eyes blazed like crystal in her white and frightened face.

'Do what, my child?' He asked the question so courteously that she almost flung the remainder of her wine full in his face.

'You know what I mean!'

'Do I?'

'You planned it!'

'What are you suggesting, Bliss?'

'The very sound of my name on your lips makes me shudder.'

'That's a pity, *moiya*, because it suits you. How well it would link itself to my name—my own middle name begins with an A. It is Adamas, which means hard as a diamond in Greek.'

Bliss was driven to her feet, but when she aimed the wine he was no longer a sitting target. Swiftly, instinctively he had moved out of range and the wine splashed across his desk and stained papers that were on it, running over a leather writing-case into his stamped initials.

In the silence Bliss's heart was a hammer that drove nails into her shrinking flesh. This time he would propose in a polite and distant voice ... this time he would tell her that if she wanted her brother to have his freedom, then she must surrender hers.

CHAPTER TWO

'WASN'T that rather a childish thing to do?' He suddenly stepped close to her and took the empty wine glass out of her grip. Bliss could feel her knees trembling beneath the silk skirt of her dress. 'You seem to share with your brother a reckless streak, my child, and reckless behaviour has to be paid for.'

'Y-you're going to make me pay, aren't you?' She backed away, feeling her spine against the edge of his desk, defiance in her eyes and the light of the desk lamp sheening her hair.

His eyes looked her up and down and she could feel herself shrinking from his threatening height and the strong shoulders that tapered to firm hips beneath the fine broadcloth that tailored his body, which hard work from an early age had packed with power. He was taller than most Greeks, which could be due to the stranger who had seduced his mother where the maquis grew wild in the Greek hills.

He was alien to everything Bliss had known. He had experienced hunger and cold and scorn, so how could it affect him if she was cold and scornful towards him? It certainly didn't show in his eyes, which trapped her in their hard amber like a palpitating moth.

'People like you,' she said, 'who run clubs like this, encourage those who can't resist gambling.'

'Really?' he drawled. 'I once heard your brother refer to you as his priggish sister.'

She flushed. 'Someone like you would know all about double dealing!'

'So you're determined to think that I put temptation in your brother's way, like a serpent?'

'It's one of the devil's guises, isn't it?' she said defiantly.

'So from being that damned Greek who took your home away from you, I have now become the devil?' He spoke sardonically and still there was no sign in his eyes that she was making him lose his temper by saying these things.

'Why did you ask Justin to run this club for you? You weren't being magnanimous, were you? You knew very well that he liked to play cards and back horses and make bets. Justin doesn't feel alive unless he's gambling, and you know it!'

'Perhaps I needed to prove something, *moiya*— that it's privilege which corrupts, not poverty.'

'If that's what you think of Justin then it makes no sense that you should want——' Bliss broke off, for she couldn't put into words what every cell in her body felt certain of.

'Are you saying that I want you?' He looked mocking. 'Do you really imagine I've been pining after you for the past two years?'

'No——' The mockery in his eyes made her skin quiver, rather like the nervy flank of a filly when the whip flicks the silky hide.

'Then what are you implying?'

'That you have Cathlamet and you want me to go with it, because I'm a St Cyr who was born there.' Bliss spoke firmly, braving his gaze. 'It's true, isn't it, Mr Apollonaris? You've made money so you want the trappings of a gentleman, and no matter what you think of my father, he was born a gentleman even if he died a gambler!'

'And you think I'm trying to reverse that order of things, that having been born a speculator I wish to become a gentleman?'

'Yes, I do think so.'

'With you as my wife, eh?'

'Nothing else would make sense.'

'So in order to achieve my ambition I laid a trap for your brother?'

'Didn't you?'

'Let us say that I—speculated.'

A sigh shook Bliss, all the way down into her body. The truth was never palatable, but at least she had it.

'Does the prospect seem so alarming to you?' As he spoke he placed his hands inside her jacket and closed them warm and strong over her hipbones. 'Are there not compensations? You won't have to work for the crystal-gazer, nor will it be necessary for you to make your clothes last until they become out of fashion. Best of all, you will be mistress of Cathlamet, and I shan't have to report your brother's embezzlement to the police. I believe the sentence for such is quite a harsh one . . . yours at my hands would be far less harsh.'

With deliberate hands he slid her lynx jacket off her shoulders and studied her in the cream silk dress that clung limpidly to her slender figure.

'You have refinement and the look of a lady,

Bliss, and because I'm a wealthy man who can afford the best, I select to have you. Do you remember the first time we met?'

'Yes,' she replied, 'I mistook you for the bailiff.'

His eyes narrowed when she said that, and then as if to punish her in the most effective way he pulled her into his arms and his breath slid warm across her cheek. 'Be warned, *moiya*, each kick of yours will be repaid with a kiss, and you don't like the thought of my kisses, do you?'

She gazed back at him, tense and defiant ... from that day she had seen him at Cathlamet he had lurked in the shadows of her life, biding his time, planning this moment when she found herself a prisoner in his arms.

'Do I have to—marry you?' She spoke the words in a barely audible voice.

'Are you suggesting some other kind of arrangement?'

'I—I'm not experienced in these matters, Mr Apollonaris, but if what you really want is to—to sleep with me——' She forced out the words, into a silence that lasted several moments, broken by Bliss herself when his hands seemed about to crush her hipbones.

'Never,' he grated, 'speak to me in that way again!'

She flung up her lashes and found his eyes smouldering with the temper she had at last aroused ... her heart palpitated as the realisation struck her that this tough Greek had the strong sense of morality which had driven his mother from her village when she found herself pregnant with a stranger's child.

'Both Justin and I went to the devil when you came into our lives,' she told him hotly.

His answer was to carry out what he had threatened, and it was useless trying to push him away from her, for his strength reduced her to a frailty she hadn't been aware of. The muscles in his arms felt like cords around her and her mouth was the helpless recipient of his driving kiss. Bliss knew very little about responding to a man, even had she wanted to respond to Paris Apollonaris. No one she'd met and been out with had made her want what was happening to her right now . . . none of those rather callow young men had dared to break through her defences.

This man sent her defences flying, holding her locked to him with one hand in the small of her back, pressing her close to the muscular hardness and warmth of his body. His mouth released hers and now his lips were searching the soft hollows of her neck, and the more she strained to evade his lips, the more insistent they became.

Oh, let him kiss her . . . take her . . . he'd never get her to feel anything but scorn for the trap he had laid for Justin; for the trick he had played on her. She let her body sag in his arms, knowing it was said of the hunter that he enjoyed the torment of his quarry.

The dark face drew away from her and she felt his breath warm on her skin. 'You feel like ice,' he said quietly.

'Did you hope to melt me?' she asked.

'Give me time, *moiya*. We Greeks are renowned for our staying power.'

'What is the Turkish part of you renowned

for?' Close like this she could see the hard thrust of the facial bones under his brown skin, and the very look and feel of him seemed to drive the strength out of her body. How could such a man be stopped from getting what he wanted? It was Greek lore, as Justin had said ... Paris Apollonaris always got his pound of flesh.

'Have you had a *seraglio* put in at Cathlamet?' she couldn't resist asking.

'You will find out when you come to live there, won't you?'

'You're so sure of yourself, aren't you, Mr Apollonaris?'

'I would suggest that you call me Paris now we've become more closely acquainted.'

Her eyes flashed mutiny at him. 'If I knew a way to get Justin out of your clutches, then you wouldn't get the chance to lay your hands on me!'

'That would be such a pity.' He drew his hands down her silken sides. 'I like what I feel, that you are a girl who has kept her body to herself. As I told you, Greeks don't care to marry a woman who has let herself be used ... my mother's life was unhappy because she was careless with her affections.'

'It looks as if history will be repeating itself.' Her skin quivered from his touch, and her innate sense of privacy felt affronted by these liberties he was taking, as if already he was taking possession of her.

He raised an enquiring eyebrow. 'How is that?'

'Because I expect to be just as unhappy as your mother—you can't imagine that I have any affection for you?'

'Quite so, but you have a great deal for Cathlamet, eh? You will be in residence when the roses bloom again in June. Surely that will make you happy?'

'June?' A trace of fear came into her eyes. 'That's only a few weeks away!'

'So it is.' He released her and leaned over to examine his desk calendar. 'I daresay I can find the time to be married to you in May. Does that suit you?'

Bliss stood there dumbly . . . none of this was a charade, even though it seemed like one. It was as real as the rain beating against the windows; real as the scent of smoke as Paris Apollonaris lit a cheroot and went to take a look behind the curtains at the downpour.

'I shall take you home,' he said.

'No—I can get a cab——'

'I insist.' He stood framed against the burgundy fabric just as she had seen him when she had entered this office an hour ago . . . in that hour so much had happened. He had taken command of her . . . there was no other way to think of it.

'You really mean to make me marry you, don't you?' The very words as she spoke them seemed detached from reality, and yet they were more meaningful than any words she had ever uttered.

'I gave you a choice,' he pointed out.

'You mean you're turning the screw!'

He shrugged and cheroot smoke slid from his well-defined nostrils. 'The way to get what you want from this life is to be determined, and none of us can change the way we are made. Your brother, my child, would be a winner and not a loser if he bothered to study the ways of his fellow creatures. Instead he's wrapped up in himself and selfish to the core.'

'Perhaps it's a family trait,' Bliss flung back. 'Be careful I'm not using you to get at your fortune.'

'If you were after my fortune, my child, you'd have leapt at my proposal two years ago.'

'Perhaps I hadn't learned at that time that working for one's living can be tedious. Perhaps I hadn't realised that buying a secondhand fur coat isn't quite so satisfying as being given one by a rich man.'

His eyes flicked her lynx jacket. 'The only family trait you share with your brother is your colouring, and you should look charming wrapped in champagne mink. We shall fly to Greece to be married, for I shall never be able to persuade my mother to come to England. There, the matter is settled.'

'How domineering you are!' Bliss resented every forceful inch of him, every black hair on his head, every thought going on at the back of his eyes as he appraised her. 'I suppose the buying and selling of people comes easier to a Greek! I can see it doesn't worry you that you're buying me!'

He calmly shook his head. 'You are worth every *drachma*, my child. You are a bargain at the price.'

'Damn you!' Bliss flinched from the cynicism in his eyes through the smoke of his cheroot. 'You're living proof that the devil looks after his own!'

'Who knows, perhaps he fathered me.' Paris Apollonaris gave a throaty laugh. 'The old gods and satyrs are said to walk the Greek hills, and it's obvious from the way you're looking at me that you are wondering when you'll see my cloven hoof.'

'I—I hope you won't break your word where my brother's concerned?'

'A Greek rarely breaks his word when given, Bliss. A bargain is a bargain.'

'It sounds just like a market place!'

'Would you prefer me to speak passionately to you? Would you like to be told that you remind me of that strange, moon-white lily plant that floats on the pool of the sunken garden at Cathlamet?'

Bliss stared at him, at the face that in the distant past the Greeks had stamped upon their coins. Between the wings of his white collar his metal-grey tie was faultlessly knotted, and his suit echoed that shade of grey and was like a smooth armour upon him. He wasn't handsome, for that was a slick word which the magazines applied to film stars.

Paris Apollonaris was a man who commanded.

'I—I'd like to go home,' she exclaimed. 'I want to be on my own——'

'I shall take you.' But for a few moments more he didn't move, and again Bliss felt trapped in the amber of his eyes. Made restless by his eyes, she went to the door where the handle twisted ineffectually in her grasp.

'The door will only open when I press a button under my desk.' She stood by the door as he moved to his desk, where he stubbed his cheroot in a glass tray. 'I intended to drive you home, Bliss, so stop looking as if you want to flee for you life.'

'If only I could!'

'And leave precious Justin to languish in jail? I've pressed the button, my child, so walk out now—I'm not stopping you. Walk out and be free of your commitments. It's as simple as that.'

She stared at the door and her impulse was to do exactly as he suggested . . . why shouldn't she? It wasn't as if Justin was worth the sacrifice she was expected to make. He was selfish and reckless, and he took it for granted that she'd stand by him.

But somewhere lost in the man he had grown into was the fair-haired boy with whom she had played on the moors. The boy she had gone riding with, and fished for tiddlers in the moorland streams.

'Aren't you going?'

'Y-you said you'd drive me home.' And with her face half hidden in the upturned collar of her jacket Bliss went ahead of Paris Apollonaris, down the stairs to the street where the pavements glistened with rain.

She shivered in the cold night air and felt the rain against her face as she watched the sleek Jaguar back out of the mews alongside the club. The passenger door opened and she slid into the car, feeling the leathered luxury as she sank back in her seat.

'Seat-belt,' he murmured.

She clipped it in place, feeling tethered in more ways than one.

'Has it never occurred to you that some things are inevitable?' He gave her a brief glance before steering the car into the traffic. 'Ask the crystal-gazer.'

'Her name is Madame Lilian, and there's no need to sound ironic.'

'Who's being ironic? Why do you think I named my club Cassandra? There's a strong vein of superstition in Greek people.'

'You should have named it the Club Machiavelli!'

He merely gave his brief, throaty laugh and said no more on the matter. Bliss watched the wiper blades stroking back and forth across the windscreen, cleaning off the rain that was instantly there again.

She decided that she would consult Madam Lilian ... perhaps even yet it lay in her stars to find a way of helping Justin without becoming the property of Paris Apollonaris.

Like Cathlamet, that was all she would be, another of his possessions; another status symbol for the Greek entrepreneur who had been born to a goat-girl.

'That was a deep sigh,' he murmured.

'It's been that kind of an evening, hasn't it?'

The Jaguar slid into the kerb in front of the tall house where Bliss had her small flat. 'I—I'm not going to ask you in.' She flumbled with the seat-belt, for her hands were trembling. 'I need to be on my own——'

'Bliss,' his firm hands closed on her shoulders, 'we have to make plans for the wedding, so I shall want to see you again quite soon. We'll have dinner together; I'm free on Thursday evening.'

'You seem to take it for granted that I shall be available.'

'Aren't you?' His eyes scanned her pale face, in which the heart-shaped mouth had a more poignant look than usual. Abruptly he bent his head and his lips brushed hers. 'Don't shiver like that, child!'

'If you're expecting passion, then you're in for a disappointment. I—I don't happen to feel that way.'

'All things are possible.' A sardonic note slid into his voice. 'I shall telephone about Thursday evening, and I would like you to make yourself available. If your employer requires you, then inform her that you have a prior engagement.'

The very word stabbed through Bliss. 'Please let me go in—I'm tired.'

'Worn out by a new set of emotions, eh? Well, at least you can sleep easy where your brother is concerned—I shan't have him put in prison.'

His hands released her into the cold wet night, but still his hold was upon her as she ran up the steps to the front door of the house where she lived. It wasn't until she had let herself in that he drove away.

CHAPTER THREE

BLISS had always been fascinated by the room in which Madame Lilian did her crystal gazing. The ceiling was painted with signs of the Zodiac, the scales of Libra predominating. Bliss had asked why this was so, and Madame had replied that life itself was balanced upon scales. In each person there was a measure of good and bad; in everyone's fate there was fortune and misfortune. Sometimes the scales were balanced heavily on one side or the other and this dictated the course of that person's life.

'But isn't it all supposition?' Bliss had queried at the time. 'Don't we make our own lives, for good or bad?'

'Never say such a thing to a clairvoyant,' Madame had said haughtily. 'We know better than most that our lives have a certain course to run, and though along the way we may make choices which go in opposition to the magnetic force which controls us, we suffer for making those fateful choices.'

Bliss had been younger then, and new to her job with Madame Lilian, so she had been sceptical when told these things. But after two years with the clairvoyant she had revised her opinion of those who believed in astrology, palmistry and the reading of the Tarot cards.

There was one thing Madame would never

touch or talk about, and that was the ouija-board. She declared it to be evil; a contraption that led into dark places.

Madame's crystal ball was of beryl rather than clear crystal, and it stood on a special mount on a white-clothed table. The frame of the mount was of ivory engraved with mystic names and symbols, and the table was circular and stood upon a pentacle of five stars laid into the floor itself. On the table stood a pair of antique candlesticks and incense burned in a far corner of the room and its effect was slightly tranquillising.

These might be the trappings of magic, the aids to an atmosphere which induced clients to believe in the fortune-telling, but nonetheless they were intriguing, and Bliss was in no doubt that her employer had impressive powers, probably a combination of extra-sensory perception and the gift of persuasion.

All of which was aided by her appearance, for she was tall and looked like a sorceress in her long jade-green gown, with chains of beads and charms about her neck. Her long, rather equine face had a strange sort of charm, and over the years Bliss had grown fond of her and enjoyed working for her.

And yet she had never asked Madame Lilian to read her fortune in the Tarot cards, with the wickedly beautiful pictures on them. She had truly felt that nothing in her life could be more shattering than finding out that Cathlamet had fallen into the hands of a stranger and she no longer had the right to live there.

Bliss had never known anyone who was Greek,

so he seemed even more enigmatic and foreign. And when the solicitor spoke his name it seemed the most outlandish name she had ever heard. Now it seemed outrageous to her, since its owner had told her that she was to share it with him. 'I—can't!' she exclaimed aloud.

'Did you speak, dear child?' Madame Lilian entered the room, chains jangling against her rather bony chest.

Bliss swung round to face Madame and there was a distracted look on her face. As the sonorous boom of Big Ben came through the window she decided to test her employer's powers of perception. She stood there, chin lifted, as the clairvoyant's jade-green eyes played over the pale luminosity of her skin and the faint smudges of violet beneath her eyes.

'My dear, you look threatened!'

'Why do you say that, Madame?' Bliss needed help and advice, though at any other time she was too private a person to seek it. Other worries and anxieties she had battled with and overcome, but now she felt herself up against a situation which she couldn't cope with on her own.

'I sense it, Bliss, very strongly.' Madame came over to where she stood and reached for her hands. 'Your skin is cold as clay, a sure sign of a very deep anxiety. It's connected with your brother, isn't it?'

'Yes.' Bliss gave a shiver. 'I'm afraid it is.'

'And it's something which needs sorting out without delay. That brother is the Knave in your house of cards, my dear Bliss. I knew that time I met him that he'd call up a demon.'

Bliss caught her breath and didn't resist when Madame drew her to the table where the beryl sphere stood covered in white silk. She sat down as Madame lit the golden candlesticks and went over to pull the curtains against the spring sunshine. 'It won't do any harm to take a look in my showing stone; doing so helps me to think, and I must try and give you the right advice.'

Madame Lilian sat down and uncovered the sphere which each night was washed in an infusion of herbs and vinegar so that it gleamed in the candlelight.

The clairvoyant had never pretended to Bliss that she saw images in the ball; what it did when she gazed into it was to create an atmosphere of auto-hypnosis. It was a form of meditation, and Bliss had been witness to some curious revelations which often sent the clients home in a mood of euphoria.

She wasn't hoping for euphoria, but she did need to be told how to cope with the demon which Justin had conjured. It had possession of her and she wanted to be told how to free herself.

'Because you have worked for me for some time,' Madame said, her gaze fixed upon the mounted ball, 'I know very well that your brother Justin has caused you other anxieties which you have quietly dealt with. But this is different, eh? Tell me of this other, more singular man.'

Bliss gave a start that seemed to jerk her heart against her breastbone. 'How do you—know?'

'Suffice it to say that I know, dear child. Describe the man.'

'Physically, do you mean?'

'No; give me an impression of his persona.'

'Well, Madame, let's say that if I kicked him in the heart, I'd need to have my foot in plaster!'

'I see.' Madam shot a look at her. 'As bad as that, eh?'

'I think so,' Bliss replied.

'He has no good points, is that what you're telling me, Bliss?'

'Well—not exactly.'

'You mean he isn't someone you'd call evil?'

'Oh no!' For some reason Bliss felt shocked by that suggestion.

'But he obviously has some kind of a hold over you, am I correct in saying so?'

Bliss inclined her head. She supposed it would be easier to spill it all out to Madame Lilian, but in a curious way she wanted the theatricality of this reading. It went with that confrontation at the Club Cassandra ... the sheer audacity of being told by Paris Apollonaris that she must marry him. She felt as if she were locked within a strange dream ... one of those dreams in which you were lost and couldn't find your way back to sanity.

'Let me see,' Madame focused her jade eyes upon the glistening sphere and all expression seemed to leave her face as she allowed her mind to wander. There was silence in the room, for Madame's flat was so close to Westminster that Big Ben was her clock. Bliss watched her and felt the beating of her heart ... now she understood why people came with their troubles to someone like Madame. A touch of magic helped when you didn't know which way to turn.

'Your brother is in debt to this man,' Madame exclaimed. 'You have to pay him back!'

Bliss raised her hands and pressed her face with them. 'How do you do it, Madame?' she gasped.

'I should be called Shirley Holmes, shouldn't I?' Madame said drily.

Bliss smiled in answer. 'After two years with you I shouldn't feel so overawed, but you've never told my fortune before.'

'Perhaps, dear child, because the fortunes of attractive young women are in their faces for everyone to read. What does this man want of you in the way of repayment?'

'How did you—guess, Madame?'

'Elementary, my dear Bliss. You have a charming but feckless brother who works where games of chance go on; it was on the cards that one day he would land himself in a serious bit of trouble and he'd expect you to bail him out. In your attempt to do so you've come up against a problem which has given you a sleepless night. It shows in the young when they haven't slept soundly; we older people look decrepit anyway. And because for young women there is a tendency for young men to loom on the horizon as the plunderers of their sleep, it didn't take too much divination.'

Madame paused and gazed directly into Bliss's eyes. 'What is it he wants of you—to make love to you?'

'More than that,' Bliss said huskily. 'He says I'm to marry him, otherwise Justin goes to jail. Justin's terrified, and I just don't know what to do— I'm at my wits' end!'

'Is the sum involved a large one?'

Bliss told her employer just how much Justin had embezzled from the club, but for some odd reason she couldn't bring herself to tell Madame Lilian the name of the man who had named his price in the private office above the club, fixing her with those amber eyes of his and looking confident that she couldn't do other than submit to his proposal.

'So he's using emotional blackmail?'

Bliss nodded.

'And yet you assert that he isn't an evil person.'

'No. He believes in retribution and he can afford to write off the sum Justin has stolen from him—so long as he gets me in exchange.'

Madame Lilian looked thoughtful and fingered the large-stoned rings on her hands. 'He's a stranger to you, dear child?'

'Not exactly.' Bliss thought of that distinctive dark face above the white shirt and metallic tie; of those strong wrists with the black hair shading the white cuffs and the masonic ovals of purest gold. Swiftly in her mind she listed his good points ... he was courteous, he had considerable style, and he had bent life to his will. He had made his way in the world, but he didn't have those awful pretensions of some people; there was no foolish air of grandeur about him, but all the saving graces couldn't cancel out the destructive one ... that he was forcing her into marriage with him, and love didn't seem to enter into the contract.

'You say not exactly,' Madame broke in on

Bliss's thoughts. 'He isn't entirely a stranger to you, then?'

Bliss shook her head.

'You aren't going to be more explicit than that, dear child? You don't intend to impart his name to me?'

'I—I'd rather not.'

'I would recognise his name, is that it?'

'You might, Madame Lilian.'

'Very well, Bliss, I shall respect your need to keep his name to yourself, but it does suggest that he's important—a personage, perhaps?'

'He's a man whose name sometimes gets into the newspapers,' Bliss admitted.

'In a business capacity.'

'Yes.'

'Then he's older than you, isn't he? Is that why you don't like the idea of marrying him?'

'He isn't years and years older than me, but I—I couldn't marry a man without love!'

'Ah, so now we arrive at the heart of the problem!' Madame Lilian sat back in her chair and her face was shadowed but for the glitter of her shrewd eyes. 'Of course, dear child, it's written all over you that you're a romantic, and that's why your feckless brother can get at your emotions. No doubt you remember him when he was a grubby-faced, mischievous little boy, but what you have to face up to is that he's now a disreputable young man who should be sent to the Colonies—if we still had them—where he could disgrace himself without involving his family. They used to do it in the old days, and it often paid off.'

Madame fell quiet for several minutes, and Bliss watched the candle flames playing their light in the ball of beryl. It began to filter into her mind what Madame Lilian was going to suggest, but where on earth would she get the fare money to send Justin out of the country?

'You borrow it, Bliss,' said Madame, reading her mind. 'You go to a reputable loan company and you ask them to lend you the cash. You then sign a contract which will request a certain amount of interest on the loan. Many people do it, dear child. It's only money—not marriage!'

'But I couldn't!' Bliss looked shocked by the idea, remembering how deeply in debt her father had sunk before his death.

'If you can't bring yourself to go to a money-lender, Bliss, then you know the alternative.'

'I—I could defy him, couldn't I?' Bliss said it without believing for a moment that she could get her own way with that man.

'A man who would break your foot if you kicked him in the heart, dear child?'

Bliss bit her lip quite painfully.

'I know of an excellent loan company which will treat you fairly,' Madame Lilian resumed. 'There's no shame in it. I've done it myself in my time, when I was starting up as a clairvoyant and I was determined to do it with style. I'm not a fake, as you know by now, but clients are impressed by a little mystification and I wanted to set up my stall in the right kind of market. It was an expensive procedure and I hadn't a bean; a friend recommended me to this loan company I've mentioned to you and I found them discreet,

extremely fair about the repayments, and they
didn't fleece me when it came to the interest on
the loan.'

She leaned forward and studied Bliss intently.
'It would be the lesser of two evils, would it not
... this man you don't want to marry and the
brother who causes you more anxiety than he's
worth! You have your own life to live and neither
of these men should be in a position to dictate to
you.'

'But I've never borrowed money in my life,'
protested Bliss, half drawn to the idea and yet
afraid of it. 'Suppose I couldn't make the repayments?'

'Now that's nonsense, Bliss.' Madame looked
slightly affronted. 'You have an excellent position
with me and I pay you a very good wage—of
course you can make the repayments. As I keep
telling you, this particular loan company has a
speckless reputation, added to which I've been on
their books as a client and my name will add
weight to your request for a loan.'

'Doesn't a woman have to be married before
she can approach one of those places?' Bliss said
doubtfully.

'Not in this day and age, dear child. Women
are persons now, not the appendages of the male
sex, even if some of them continue to imagine
that such a bondage still exists. It sounds to me as
if this magnate believes it! The cruel audacity of
it, your youth and innocence in exchange for your
brother's perfidy! He must be quite monstrous,
even if you remain charitable enough to say that
he isn't.'

'He's a man who's become accustomed to bargaining,' Bliss said, carrying in her mind an incisive image of his amber-eyed face; the warrior face that men of business acquired, especially if they enjoyed the battles and were merciless in being the victor.

'And he thinks he's made a good bargain where you are concerned?'

Bliss made a deprecating gesture. 'I'm not such a bargain—he's in no doubt about my feelings for him; he knows they aren't in the least flattering!'

'That wouldn't trouble him if he's as hard as you say he is.' Madame looked down the slope of her nose. 'With the situation the way it is, he'll make a slave of you, and the whip he'll hold over you is that he bought you with the money your brother took from him. You'll never feel proud again, you realise that?'

'Of course I realise it.' Bliss thrust a hand through her hair which felt heavy against her aching head. 'I—I feel as if I'm caught up in a bad dream, none of it seems as if it could be real, but it is!'

'That's why, without alarming my clients, I never disabuse them of the notion that the devil is among us and always ready to stir up some hell. I sense strongly that this man is a foreigner, for there is an aura of darkness about you, Bliss, as of someone who casts a long dark shadow. You must not fall under his influence, do you hear me. You will be lost!'

'Oh, please,' Bliss looked frightened, 'don't tell me all this——'

'It's for your own good, dear child. You are a young woman who needs to be loved, not *owned*. Slavery went out of the Western world with Abraham Lincoln.'

'Then what am I to do, because he's going to want his answer on Thursday evening?'

'This is what you will do.' Madame rose to her feet and went to the large old sideboard where her handbag lay. She opened it and took out a wallet which held a selection of cards, pasteboard ones on which were printed business addresses and telephone numbers. Finally she found what she was searching for and brought the card to Bliss, somewhat dog-eared and redolent of the peach face-powder which was always floating loose in the big leather handbag.

'Go and see these people,' Madame instructed. 'Take this afternoon off, Bliss, and borrow sufficient cash to pay for your brother to go by ship to Australia. Now that is a tough country and it might make a man of him. Book the passage yourself, otherwise he might spend the money. Make it a ship, because jet planes arrive at their journey's end a little too soon, and from what you've told me of this magnate, he's in a position to have various airports watched for your brother's arrival. He'll have him scooped back in the net, and that is what you want to avoid, isn't it, dear child?'

Bliss nodded and stared at the company name on the card her employer had given her. She hated the thought of approaching them for this loan, yet what Madame Lilian suggested was a feasible way out for Justin and herself. Justin would jump at the idea. He'd do anything to avoid arrest and imprisonment, and though it was possible that Paris Apollonaris would check the passenger lists of outgoing ships and could have Justin put under arrest by the captain, she had a feeling that he wouldn't do it.

She knew instinctively that he didn't so much want Justin behind bars, he wanted possession of her, and Justin's misdemeanour gave him the means.

'She who hesitates, Bliss,' Madame murmured.

'I—I've no choice really, have I?' Bliss clenched the card in her fingers.

'Two birds with one stone, dear child.'

Bliss nodded. If Justin went to Australia then he might land on his feet, and in any case he couldn't cause her the kind of anxiety she was going through right now. There would be half the world between them, and she would be in a position to tell Paris Apollonaris what he could do with his proposal of marriage.

She felt a tiny shaft of regret at the thought of Cathlamet, but after all, it was only a house, a building of brick and stone . . . a prison, in fact, if she returned there with a husband who looked upon her as something he had bought.

Bliss rose to her feet with decision. 'I'm going to do it,' she said, 'I think I'd rather be in hock to these people than in hock to—to the man I told you about. They can't be any more ruthless than he is!'

'That's the spirit, Bliss!' Madame Lilian gave a nod of approval 'Now make a pot of coffee while I telephone P&O and find out for you if there's a vessel about to depart for Australia or some other far place, and what a single berth will cost. That brother of yours has caused you more trouble than he's worth!'

'I am doing the right thing?' Bliss still looked troubled.

'It's written!' exclaimed the clairvoyant.

CHAPTER FOUR

THE telephone rang in an imperative way and Bliss felt her nerves jangle in tune with the sound. She had just climbed out of the bath and as she hastened to the telephone she fastened the sash of her towelling wrap.

'Hello?'

'We have Elias Mercantile on the line, Miss St Cyr. The managing director wishes to have a word with you.'

Bliss felt her heart jump against her breastbone. Elias Mercantile was the loan company to which she had applied for a loan of several hundred pounds which had been granted to her after she had given Madame Lilian as her guarantor and signed a contract to the effect that she would pay back the loan in monthly instalments which, to her relief, hadn't been too steep.

'Is anything wrong——?' Bliss suddenly felt a sense of chill and she drew her wrap closer about her damp body.

'You sound nervous.' The voice was deep and rather grating, and there was a foreign inflection which caused her to sway and grab the edge of the telephone table.

'I hope you haven't fainted!'

Bliss stared at the handset ... it just wasn't possible that two men could speak in exactly the same tone and manner, and the telephone operator had said distinctly that the managing director of Elias Mercantile wished to speak to her.

'Who am I speaking to?' she asked breathlessly.

'I'm hardly flattered that you don't recognise my voice, Bliss, especially in view of our very special relationship.'

Paris Apollonaris? But it couldn't be!

'It is,' he said, right against her eardrum.

'You—you manage Elias Mercantile?' she managed to say.

'Lock, stock and barrel, as the saying goes in this country.'

'Oh no!'

'Elias, my child, has another name in Greek, and that is Apollo, and had you been a better classics scholar at your very expensive school in Bucks you might have put two and two together. It isn't that I profess to resemble the Greek god Apollo, but it is part of my surname. Quite a quirk of destiny, eh, that you should choose to borrow from my company the money to send your brother out of my reach.'

At least Justin was out of his reach, for as luck would have it there had been a cancellation on a P&O vessel for Singapore, and Justin had leapt at the chance of leaving his troubles behind him. It hadn't bothered him in the least that Bliss had set aside her principles and borrowed the money on his behalf. He had hugged the breath out of her, then had dashed off to throw belongings into a bag and grab a train for Southampton.

'I'll drop you a postcard,' he had said, and had left her to have this bombshell dropped on her.

Bliss realised that her brother must have known that Elias Mercantile was one of the companies owned and operated by Paris Apollonaris.

The very reputable and reliable company so highly recommended by Madame Lilian, who had failed to see in her crystal ball the tripwire lying in wait for Bliss.

'Did you imagine,' said Bliss, pulling herself together with an effort, 'that I was going to tamely accept your proposal of marriage, on your terms?'

'Imagination doesn't come into it,' he rejoined. 'I think I warned you that when a Greek strikes a bargain his word is his pledge. Admitted, it's a little upsetting for you that you came to my company for the loan which has assisted your brother in getting out of the country. You worked fast, child. I admire your spirit, but you have to agree, in all fairness, that you are more in my debt than ever.'

Damn him! Bliss wanted to slam down the handset and join Justin in running away, but her character was different from his and she saw the justice in what Paris Apollonaris said to her.

'You have my sympathy, Bliss. So disappointing for you that the oracle for whom you work failed to see my name spelled out in her crystal ball. I'm aware that she's been a client of Elias Mercantile, so I assume it was she who made the suggestion that you approach a loan company. I don't think you'd have thought of doing so without some urging.'

'Yes,' Bliss admitted. 'Madame Lilian thought it would be a way out for me.'

'Didn't she read the Tarot cards?' he mocked.

'Y-you're a devil!' she exclaimed. 'Your luck is really of a diabolical kind, isn't it?'

'If you say so, Bliss.' He gave the laugh that wasn't really a laugh at all, more an expression of a very sardonic sense of humour. 'You and I have matters to discuss, so I shall arrive at your flat in about an hour in order to take you to dinner. Be ready, won't you?'

There was a click, then came the purring sound that indicated he had rung off. Bliss cradled the telephone and walked on uncertain legs to the couch where she sank down and gripped a cushion between her hands, needing something to cling to while she absorbed the realisation that she was still entangled in the web spun by her impecunious brother.

From the very start she had had a fateful kind of feeling that she wasn't going to elude Paris Apollonaris, and it no longer surprised her that he owned a loan company as well as a gaming club. It was easy enough to see that he wasn't a conventional man, and that he enjoyed involving himself in projects that teetered on the edge of danger. That he made money from such projects added spice to the game.

Bliss could well imagine his sardonic amusement upon learning that she had become a client of his loan company, in all her naïve innocence!

Now he really held a whip over her, this tough Greek who had long since learned not to care very much about being liked so long as he was feared. He had grown up hardened against people, having found out that they could be cruel to a child just because that child lacked a father.

Inch by inch his armour had spread and hardened until now it encased him to the heart. Nothing could penetrate to that organ, he made sure of that.

He was impregnable, Bliss told herself . . . but she wasn't!

An hour, he had said. He was coming to her flat and he had obviously made up his mind that she was going to marry him whether she wanted to or not.

And as he had stated, she was more in debt to him than ever. She had played directly into his hands and her only weapon was a show of dignity. She had always prided herself on a certain composure and dignity and she would meet him with her head held high instead of the bowed-down demeanour that he probably expected to find when he arrived.

She went into the bedroom and took a look at the dresses in the built-in cupboard. She took out the black crystal-pleated with a frill of white around the neck. She would wear this and he'd get the message. She had nothing to celebrate in the contemplation of marriage to a man who thought in terms of money and gain rather than love.

Black suited her because she was so fair in colouring. She took her long swathe of silvery-gilt hair and carefully knotted it at her nape. She lightly painted her mouth and clipped small pearl studs to her earlobes. She studied her reflection and saw the apprehension that made the pupils of her eyes wide and dark against the grey irises.

She saw what it was that Paris Apollonaris wanted—her fair looks in contrast to his own Grecian darkness. Her lineage in compensation for his unknown source; even her rebellion in which fear showed its glitter there in her eyes above the refined nose, the heart-shaped mouth and oval chin.

Long, long ago the Norman knight who had built Cathlamet upon land given to him for his part in the siege of York had forced into marriage with him the daughter of a Saxon knight. Bliss's father had taken her, when still a small child, to a church in York and shown her the stained window in which the Saxon wife of the Norman conqueror knelt upon her *prie-dieu*. Even then Bliss had seen a resemblance to herself in the extreme fairness she had inherited, the Saxon genes at war with the Norman ones in producing every so often offspring with silver-gilt hair and light grey eyes.

Bliss was neither vain nor mock-modest, and she knew deep inside herself that Paris Apollonaris admired the look of her and was quite determined to have her.

She caught her breath, because there was every possibility that he knew the story of the Saxon girl who had been carried to Cathlamet on the saddlebow of an armoured Norman, and it was the kind of story that would appeal to a man who had set out to conquer his own poor beginnings and by his manipulation of money make people come to him as suppliants.

That was why he enjoyed owning a finance company with its credit facilities, Bliss decided.

He liked having people at his mercy, as she was at his mercy. It was a realisation that sent the rebel blood racing through her veins, so that when he buzzed for admittance there was a wild flush in her cheeks when she opened the door.

He stepped inside her sitting-room, and always it came as something of a shock, the lean dark height of him, those lion-coloured eyes sweeping over her as if he already owned her . . . which in a way she supposed he did.

'How extremely attractive you look, *moiya*.' He came and stood within inches of her slender figure in the black dress offset with the white neck frill. Bliss instinctively backed away, fearing that he was going to seal his ownership with a kiss.

'Don't panic,' he murmured, 'I won't spoil your make-up or mess up your hair—not right now. Pin this to your wrap.'

He handed her a box with a transperent lid and she stared at the spray of small, perfect orchids which lay inside. 'Th-thank you.' She lifted off the lid, glad to be able to concentrate on the flowers so she wouldn't have to meet his eyes. She drew out the orchids, then gave a gasp at finding fastened among them a jewelled brooch in the shape of a butterfly.

Her gaze flew to his face. 'You shouldn't——!'

'It didn't cost the earth,' he mocked. 'And it's perfectly respectable for a girl to accept a trinket from her fiancé—that hasn't changed, you realise?'

'I'd hoped——' She bit her lip as she stabbed her finger with the pin of the brooch.

'Serves you right,' he said unkindly. 'This is your wrap?' He picked up the lynx jacket which she had worn the other evening and eyed it with a faint frown. 'I shall buy you mink, as I promised.'

'I'm fond of the jacket,' she said defensively. 'I came upon it in a secondhand boutique and took to it right away. I don't want mink coats!'

'We shall see.' He took orchids and brooch from her nervous hands and firmly pinned the spray to the jacket with the brooch whose jewels were a scintillating mixture of deep blue, a dash of gold and a hint of green. The gem sparkled as Paris swung the jacket about her shoulders.

'Don't you ever take no for an answer?' she asked, chin tilted as she looked up at him. The top of her fair head came to his hard and stubborn jaw, and it went through her mind that he was so—so emphatically a man.

'Not if I can help it,' he replied. 'Surely you have to agree that a rich husband is better than an impecunious one, for love in a garret might sound all right in a magazine story, but in reality it means going cold and hungry a good deal of the time, and love soon dies where there is rising damp and a smell of boiled cabbage on the stairs.'

'I—I'm sure real love can overcome a lot of difficulties,' she said, though her nose had wrinkled of itself at the mention of the smell of boiled cabbage, a vegetable she couldn't abide and which one of the tenants in this house was fond of cooking.

'In theory a lot of things seem possible, my child, but in practice love like the roses will only flourish in the warm sunlight. Permit me to speak from experience about poverty.' Suddenly his words sounded as if chipped from a block of stone. 'I saw for myself how the kind and loving side of my mother was hardened by a hard life. She was a mere girl when she made the mistake of finding some warmth in a man's arms, and she was never allowed to forget that mistake, because I arrived as a result of it.'

'Is that why you don't like many people?' asked Bliss, feeling a stab of sympathy for the boy he had been but unable to feel in any way softened by the hard and forceful adult he had grown into. He didn't wear the visual armour of a Norman knight, but he certainly had a tough skin and an iron opinion of people.

'Is it necessary to like people?' He looked sardonic. 'There are some I respect for their acumen, some I admire for their appearance, some I thoroughly despise for their narrow minds. I am only a human being, *moiya*, it's that circumstances have made me less prone to being hypocritical. I don't suffer from the social disease of saying nice things to people's faces, and twisting a knife in their characters when they turn their backs. In short, Bliss, I don't wear a polite mask while thinking poisonous thoughts.'

'For a Greek speaking English you have a very good vocabulary, Mr Apollonaris.' His accent, in fact, tinged his words with many shades of meaning, and Bliss was quite certain that he wore a mask, though admittedly not one of those that smiled falsely.

'I am going to insist that you call me by my

first name.' Abruptly he had hold of her by her
fur-clad shoulders and she felt in him the
strength that could have swung her clear off her
feet. 'If you want the truth, then the truth is that
I do consider that I own you as I own Cathlamet.
You belong there, you always have, not in this
run-down boarding-house in Earls Court, redolent of other people's cooking and the sounds of
their radios and their arguments.'

His grip tightened on her, possessively. 'For
heaven's sake, you little fool, don't you know that
I promised your father there would always be
room for you at Cathlamet? In many ways he was
a foolish and reckless man, but you he loved, and
it tore him apart that you were being deprived of
your home. Do you imagine I would hold on to
that great stone mansion on the moors if it were
not for you?'

Bliss stared up at the dark grim face and her
heart thudded in her breast. 'I—I knew that was
why you proposed to me before. I knew it was on
your conscience——'

'Conscience be damned!' He gathered her
hurtfully into his arms and his lips took hers
apart savagely, his hot breath searing into her,
making her aware as never before that he was a
taker, a conqueror, a man just like the first one to
set foot on the threshold of Cathlamet as lord and
master of the domain.

When Paris finally let go her lips Bliss was too
dazed to say anything ... too breathless for
words, held and owned by a man who wouldn't,
this time, allow her to throw back his proposal in
his face.

'Not on my conscience,' he murmured. 'On my senses. You are the wife I want, and you are the wife I'm going to have.'

'Even if I don't love you?' she flung breathlessly into his face.

'Story-book love?' he mocked. 'That passion of twin souls in harmony? What we feel, Bliss, we feel with the body, not some mystic organ which the laboratory technician has never managed to find inside a single man or woman. Our urges are of the flesh, and what is wrong with that?'

As he spoke he stroked a hand over her hair and let his fingertips glide around her neck, fastening a hand that held her lightly but securely.

'Don't tell me,' he said, his voice pitched even deeper, 'that you feel nothing when I touch you. At this very moment I feel your pulse beating at my fingertips.'

'Our hearts race when we're frightened——' And held like this, so close to him, Bliss was very aware of her own inexperience where any man was concerned, let alone Paris Apollonaris in whom temper and passion were fired by Greek and Turkish elements. There it was for her to see in the savage definition of his features beneath the tautly-drawn, sun-darkened skin.

'So I frighten you, eh?' He seemed to relish the thought; it lit a fierce little smile in his eyes. 'Perhaps you are merely hungry, my child, and I have reserved for us a table for two at the Ruby Tower, a Greco-Turkish restaurant where the lamb chops melt in the mouth. Come, let us be off to our dinner!'

Down in front of the house, parked on yellow lines, was the dark-bodied Jaguar whose palatial interior was upholstered in grey hide. 'My favourite colour.' said Paris, looking deep into Bliss's eyes.

Her heart jolted, for she realised that in his fashion he was paying court and saying the kind of things that an Englishman would feel inhibited about saying.

Until now she hadn't given much thought to courtship and wedding bells ... was there a ringing of bells at a Greek marriage? She felt quite certain that Paris Apollonaris would insist on a Greek ceremony.

'*I'm going to be married to this man!*' The sentence rang through her mind and sent panic signals racing through her body. '*He thinks my love for Cathlamet will make up for that lack of love between us!*'

'Do you like Greek food?' The car purred at some traffic signals, the ruby glow reflecting into the Jaguar.

'I've never tried any;' she replied, her fingers gripping the seat belt that fastened her beside him.

'Then you have a treat in store.' The car started foward again, heading into a quieter section of the West End. Paris drove as he did everything, with determination and precision and not a sign of nerves. Bliss didn't feel particularly hungry, not even when they arrived at the restaurant and were met by delicious aromas.

They were led by the head waiter to a secluded table set with glimmering lamps, directly beneath a striking Greek mural that decorated the wall, that of a charioteer holding with firmness and grace a team of prancing horses.

Bliss stared at the face in the mural and saw the definition of feature, the power and confidence which was reflected in the face of the man sharing the table with her.

'I'm going to suggest that you eat Greek,' he said persuasively.

'Then you had best order for me.' She didn't attempt to display any interest in the menu. 'I'll leave it up to you—as you've taken over my life.'

'What a very dramatic statement!' he mocked. 'There are young women who would be delighted to be wined and dined at a place such as this.'

'Then it's a pity you aren't with one of them,' she rejoined. 'I don't intend to be dazzled by you or this restaurant, if that's what you were hoping for.'

'I hope for nothing that I can't get for myself, *moiya*.' He gave his attention to the menu and when the waiter came he ordered their courses in Greek, the dark and powerful consonants coming more naturally to him than the English which he spoke with more deliberation.

'So what kind of mischief do you suppose your brother will get up to when he reaches Singapore?'

Bliss stared across at her self-imposed fiancé and felt as a moth must feel when it finds itself trapped in a web, its wings breaking on the cunning strands.

'I—I think you're in league with the devil,' she said.

'My child, am I not the son of the goat-god himself?' Paris gazed at her with a sardonic glint of amusement in his eyes. 'Isn't that what you believe in preference to the simple truth?'

'Do you know the meaning of the word?' she asked.

'There are two kinds of entrepreneur, you know.' He broke a bread-stick with a snap. 'Those who use confidence tricks, and those whose confidence needs no trickery. I'm involved in a number of companies, having many irons in the fire, as you British have it, and not one of those irons is in any way bent. You hate me because of Cathlamet, but I assure you the mortgage came into my hands quite legally; your father needed money and I am in the business of supplying it. Unfortunately a good deal of the money found its way across the roulette table, thereby leaving your father with the necessity to borrow again in order to pay his gambling debts. I allowed him to use my club because he would only have gone to another which might have been run less honestly.'

He held her gaze, his will overpowering hers in that long and dominating look. 'If I had a daughter, Bliss, I would build for her, not make her homeless, so lay a little of the blame on your father. It was he who gambled away your home.'

'Because men such as you run places where men can gamble their lives away!'

'I don't usually encourage the kind of customer that your father was.'

'Really?' Bliss felt herself flushing beneath his gaze, for there was no denying her father's feverish addiction to games of chance. 'Why did you allow him through your doors if you disapproved of him so much?'

'I think you know the answer to your own question, Bliss.'

'Do I?' she fenced.

'I saw your father throwing away his heritage across a green baize table and I wondered how he could do such a thing. I'd watch him, almost with fascination. Night after night he would come to the Cassandra, looking the perfect gentleman, and leaving each time a little more of his history there among the cards and the dice. Men like myself don't create the gamblers; they need places where they can go to perdition, and I was a man without a heritage, who had made up his mind to make money.'

He steepled his long, strong fingers. 'Do you want to know how I became owner of the Cassandra?'

'If you want to tell me.' Bliss infused no note of interest into her voice, but inwardly she wanted to know, because the Club Cassandra had been a sort of second home to her father.

'I had a boatload of denim bound for China and I traded it for the club, and when I took it over I found that Geoffrey St Cyr was already deep in debt there. I thought him a confounded fool, but I liked him. English gentlemen are easy to like.'

'Unlike Greeks,' she murmured.

'I wonder,' he murmured, 'if one day you will say something nice to the man you are going to marry?'

'Don't you mean the man who is going to force me to marry him?'

'Cracking a whip, like that charioteer?' He gestured at the mural. 'Hasn't it occurred to you that by marrying me you'll be regaining all the things that your father threw away?'

'What a very mercenary mind you have, Mr Apollonaris.' Bliss infused a look of scorn into her eyes. 'You must worship money!'

'I respect it.' His eyes and his features looked bronze-hard, then he dug a hand into his jacket and drew out something from an inner pocket. He slid it across the table to her. 'Try that on for size; once you start wearing it you might start using my first name.'

'What is it?' She gazed at the small square box, knowing very well what was inside.

'Open it and see.'

'I—I don't think I want to.'

'Then let me open it for you.' He took back the box and exposed the ring in its satin bed, twin smouldering rubies cupped in gleaming gold. 'Diamonds are cold in their brilliance, emeralds are somehow showy and opals are said to bring bad luck, so I chose rubies, which glow like flames. Hold out your left hand!'

Instead she clenched it in her lap, defying his lion-coloured eyes. He couldn't force her to accept the ring in a public restaurant with other people looking on ... could he? Bliss was too unsure of him to be certain.

CHAPTER FIVE

THE gems of the ring burned like fire in the palm of his hand, so unflawed in contrast to the flaws in their relationship. 'There are certain things we have to do, Bliss, and one of them is that you must wear my ring. It will look stunning against your white skin, and no woman who is truly feminine is without a touch of vanity. Come, do as you are told.'

'I—I'm not a child——'

'Then stop behaving like one.'

'I don't like wearing rings—they fidget me.'

'You are going to have to get used to this one, so you might as well make a start—hold out your hand to me!'

His voice and look had become more insistent, and he didn't seem to care in the least that people at an adjoining table had suspended their conversation in order to listen to him. Embarrassment and not desire drove Bliss to obey him, his left hand holding hers as he slid the beautiful ring into place.

'There, child, did that hurt?'

'It hurts my pride,' she rejoined.

'Too bad that you think so.' He shrugged and shifted his attention to the wine waiter who had brought the bottle of Bollinger he had ordered. The waiter withdrew the bottle from the ice-bucket and holding it in a napkin he showed Paris the label. Paris nodded his approval.

'The wine is the same age as my fiancée,' he remarked.

The waiter glanced at Bliss and with a smile replied to Paris in Greek. After he had pulled the cork and filled the flutes, Bliss felt curious enough to ask what the man had said.

Paris raised his flute and studied the sheen of the wine through the crystal, the minuscule bubbles flickering at the rim of the glass. 'He said that I was a fortunate man if my fiancée was as sweet as the wine.'

She flushed slightly. 'Too bad for you that I'm not.'

'That's a matter of opinion.'

'Do I look a picture of joy?' she scoffed. 'I'm going along with all this because I have no choice. I'm sitting here with you, wearing your ring, because you've trapped me, and no creature that's trapped wants to lick the hand of the trapper.'

'You misunderstand my aspirations, Bliss. I don't want you fawning all over me.'

'What do you want, then?' She dared to ask, dared to look right into his eyes, dared him to answer her.

'Exactly what I have.'

'Oh, and what is that?'

'You,' he said simply. '*Yasas!*' He put his wine glass to his lips and drank deeply of the wine, and Bliss was made to feel as if he were drinking deeply of her lips and her body. Her eyes looked at him wildly, at the strong outline of his shoulders beneath the jacket that was darkly severe and superbly cut, his shirt-front strikingly white against his skin which from his infancy had been exposed to the hot Greek sun. Not only had the sun burned itself into him, but when he lowered his glass she saw that his lips were compressed as if from the taste of bitter memories.

'My decisions are never swayed by sentiment,' he told her. 'It's just as well that you know it.'

'You're swayed by a need for revenge.' Never had she been more certain of anything, and it made her sips of wine taste bitter.

'Revenge may be wicked,' he agreed, 'but the impulse is a very natural one.'

'Even though I've taken nothing from you?' she asked.

He studied her intently as she sat there facing him in the gold-shaded lamplight of their table, her hair a silvery frame about her pensive, finely boned face in which her grey eyes glimmered as if with tiny frozen tears.

'Don't be sure that you've taken nothing from me, *moiya*.'

'What could I have taken?' She looked astounded. 'We've met less than half a dozen times.'

'Quite!' He spoke curtly, and his gaze had switched to a woman at a nearby table, whose dress was designed so that the cleft between her breasts was a deep valley down which the eyes of any could stray.

'A woman's body is meant for intimacy, not public display.' Though Paris spoke in English his intonation was purely Greek, and when his eyes returned to Bliss they swept her dress with the approval of the Greek in whom were whispers of the Turkish *seraglio*.

Their first course arrived, tender slices of smoked fish served with tiny pickled aubergines, sliced artichoke hearts and large juicy olives, accompanied by twisted hoops of sesame bread.

'We call this bread *kalouria*.' Paris broke a piece and put it between his hard white teeth; he chewed it appreciatively. 'It's baked fresh every day and doesn't come in plastic packets which have been in the freezer. It's no wonder that Western people are becoming rather plastic in their emotions and their behaviour. Bread when it's good is the staff of life.'

Bliss ate her food and realised once again that the Greek she had become so involved with (quite against her will), had a way of expressing himself that was individual and unconcerned about people's reaction to his opinions. Speaking in the popular idiom would never occur to him. Saying the kind of things that people expected to hear would go against the grain of him. Being in line, falling in step, becoming traumatic if he wasn't liked, these were not important to Paris Apollonaris.

'I suppose,' Bliss took a steadying sip of wine, 'you'll insist on a Greek wedding?'

'It was never in question, *pedhi mou*.' He gave a snap of his fingers and when the waiter came briskly he ordered some more of the delicious bread.

'I,' Bliss nervously sliced her fish, 'I hope it isn't a long and complicated ceremony?'

He shook his dark head. 'It's a rather beautiful one, and of course it will be performed in Greece.'

'Greece!' Bliss looked at him with a flash of resistance in her eyes. 'Oh, but surely there are churches in this country where we can be— married?'

'Doubtless,' he agreed, 'but I wish my mother to attend my marriage, and she will never travel to this country to do so. You will like my country; at least the sun will be shining.'

'You want everything your way, don't you?' Resentment crept into Bliss's eyes. 'You have a monumental ego!'

'So?' He shrugged his shoulders. 'Who is there in England for you to really care about—a few distant relations? I care a great deal for my mother and it will give her pleasure to come to our wedding; it will make up for what she never had herself, surely you see that? Come, you aren't a selfish person, Bliss.'

'No,' she agreed. 'I wouldn't be in this fix if I put myself first all the time.'

'You say such flattering things to your fiancé,' he mocked. 'So you regard yourself as being in a fix, an English way of saying you are in a situation you can't get out of, eh?'

'Obiously you aren't going to let me out of it.'

'Like Pearl White tied to the railway lines?' He gave his rather grating laugh. 'Always at the last moment she is released from bondage, eh? I may not be a hero in a white stetson, *moiya*, but I'm not altogether a villain—won't you believe that?'

'I'm not a heroine,' she rejoined. 'The unknown happens to make me nervous.'

'Come, if that were true then you wouldn't work for a clairvoyant, the renowned Madame Lilian.'

'It amuses you, of course. You think it's a lot of tosh, don't you, just because she steered me to your darned money-lending establishment?'

'Don't make me out as made of brass entirely, Bliss. We Greeks are a very superstitious race of people and we have our own Delphic oracle, and there are village girls who still keep up certain quaint traditions relating to love. Girls will be girls and they like to know if a dominant male is going to come along who will make their lives rapturous. Does Madame Lilian have clients of that type?'

'Now and again,' Bliss admitted. 'I was sceptical of her powers in the beginning, but now I'm less so.'

'Despite her failure to see my visage looming in her crystal ball?'

'Your influence was there, probably controlling her.' Even as Bliss spoke the words she realised that there might be some truth in them. A clairvoyant, by reason of her calling, laid herself open to all kinds of influence, and Bliss was discovering that the man who sat opposite to her in this gold-shadowed dining-room had a very powerful aura. It lay not only in his features and his build, but was there in his eyes, the pupils and lashes so densely black in contrast to the golden irises.

The empty plates of their first course were

whisked away and the trolley arrived on which a large joint of lamb was crackling in its own fat and juices surrounded by a selection of vegetables. The succulent look of the meat suddenly aroused Bliss's appetite, and she didn't object when the waiter sliced an ample portion of the lamb and placed it on her plate, adding a couple of kidneys and baked potatoes, cauliflower and carrots.

'Gravy, madam?'

'Please.' And as she watched the hot dark gravy being poured over her dinner Bliss wasn't unaware that her host was watching her, probably amused in his sardonic way by her sudden show of appetite.

'Do go ahead and start,' he said to her. 'Food should be enjoyed while it's hot—like some of our other appetites.'

But she waited for him to be served with his food, innately polite, her face coolly composed and hiding any sign that his remark had pierced that deep inner centre which she hadn't been fully aware of until his recent advent into her life. Bliss didn't pretend to be experienced where men were concerned, but she was warned by her instincts that Paris Apollonaris was a man whose sensual drives were probably on a level with his ambitions.

As she cut into her meat the rubies burned and gleamed on her hand, very much another sign that Paris meant their marriage to be a real one and not some sort of legal pretence.

'You like lamb?' he asked.

'When it isn't sacrificial,' she found herself replying.

'Ah, a reference to yourself, no doubt?'

'I am a sacrificial lamb, aren't I?'

'Appetisingly served up with flaxen hair, unawakened eyes and a slimly inviting body,' he agreed, meeting her eyes as he placed a portion of lamb in his mouth.

Bliss felt the warning heat of a blush and quickly lowered her eyes as she placed food on her fork. Openly now he was letting her know that he intended to exact full repayment of the debt which Justin had incurred. Oh, if only she were more experienced, one of those girls who had been around with men and acquired that brash look which Paris in his experience would be quick to notice. But he knew, darn his eyes, that she was inexperienced. It lay in her eyes for him to see, otherwise he wouldn't be eager to marry her but would probably suggest a less respectable arrangement.

When they were ready for dessert Paris didn't ask for the sweet trolley to be wheeled to their table. Instead the waiter came with plates on which hot cranberries spilled from pastry straight from the oven.

With thick cream poured from a silver jug the pie was mouthwatering, and Bliss said so.

'I'm pleased you like it,' he smiled. 'Most of our meal has been Greek, but not this sweet. I was introduced to it by an American friend, and the chef here at the Ruby Tower always makes it for me when I come to dine. So at last, *moiya*, we have something in common, a sweet tooth for cranberries and cream. You'll be pleased to hear that the cook I've installed at Cathlamet can also bake cranberry pie to perfection; it was one of the requirements of the position.'

'What became of Sarah who used to cook for my father?' Bliss felt a stab of regret and pain as she spoke. remembering the great warm kitchen with its ceiling-high dresser lined with crockery and pans, the long scrubbed table with its deep drawers, the huge old cooking range and the hanging lamps attached to hooks in the white-washed ceiling.

How she longed to see the house again, but when she did it would be as the wife of a man she barely knew. He wasn't easy to know . . . she felt that strange and alien impulses prowled through his veins.

'She didn't wish to cook for me,' Paris shrugged his well-clad shoulders, 'so I pensioned her off and I believe she went to live with her daughter. You will, of course, find certain changes; it's inevitable. I have a new man in charge of the stables and there are fresh horses in the stalls. Some parts of the house have been refurbished, but that in no way interferes with its ambience. I have quite good taste, you know.'

As Paris spoke his eyes swept Bliss's hair and face, overtly letting her know that he considered her an example of his good taste. She should have felt flattered, she supposed, but whenever he looked at her she felt that he was thinking of her in terms of a good bargain. She fitted in with his concept of ownership; she belonged at Cathlamet and was as much a part of the place as its Yorkstone walls which were always swept clean by the rain, and the towers that presided over its slate roofs and mullioned windows.

And then, quite suddenly, a very alarming thing took place in the mellow dining-room of the Ruby Tower ... a diner at one of the adjacent tables started to choke on something he'd swallowed, while his female companion sat petrified while he made awful noises and grew puce in the face.

Paris took one look, thrust back his chair and strode over to the distressed man. Quickly and firmly he tilted the man's head back, pushed a finger down his throat and dislodged the item that was choking him. Within about three minutes the man was breathing more easily and the puce colour was fading from his face, leaving it rather ashen instead.

Then as Bliss watched, almost holding her own breath, the man's companion leapt to her feet, ran to Paris and flung her arms about his neck. He lowered his head and spoke a few words, then put her firmly away from him. As he came back to Bliss she found herself wondering how he could do a thing like that. Everyone else had sat staring at the man, either feeling helpless or alarmed, but without a moment's hesitation Paris had acted.

His very confidence seemed to take her breath away, and all she could do was look at him as he sat down and calmly resumed drinking his coffee.

'It was a piece of fruit,' he told her. 'A segment of an orange—see, they are leaving now. I told his wife to take him to hospital just in case I had scratched his throat with my finger nail. In my class at school, many years ago, a child almost choked on a piece of orange and in dislodging it the teacher did scratch him and the child developed an infection which caused an abscess.'

'You,' he made her feel at a loss, somehow, 'you're a very unexpected man, Paris.'

'You think so?' His smile came and went. 'At last you have spoken my first name, which I didn't expect for some time.'

Bliss hadn't realised that his name had slipped out, and right away she was on the defensive again. 'You take command,' she exclaimed. 'I don't think you're a bit concerned that you're taking over my life—as if I've nothing to give up that measures up to your achievements. I prefer to work for my living—I don't want to be your household pet!'

'Nonsense.' He pushed towards her a dish containing sweets such as Turkish delight, fondants and raisin fudge. 'Have a piece of delight, *moiya*. I'm sure at your age that you don't need to watch your weight, and if you do, then don't let it worry you. The Turk in me quite likes a rounded limb.'

'It would!' Her eyes raced over his face in a desperate search for some hint that he could be persuaded to take back his ring and release her from what she could only see as a kind of bondage. It was proof that she meant nothing to him as a person that he swept aside her entreaties in such a casual way. He wasn't concerned to please her . . . he just wanted to possess her.

'A—a woman is no more to you than a pleasure!' she accused.

'Quite.' He flung a piece of fudge between his

white teeth and chewed it with obvious enjoyment.

'You don't even bother to deny it,' she said, aghast.

'I never do bother to deny the truth, *pedhi mou.*'

'Oh——' Bliss was lost for words, and snatching up her evening purse she pushed back her chair and got to her feet, 'I'm going to the powder-room—and I hope you choke on your darned sweets!'

Upon reaching the powder-room she found that she was trembling with a mixture of temper and tears. She brushed them away angrily—there seemed no way out of his grasp, and even if she dashed out of the Ruby Tower and ran off into the night she would eventually have to return to her flat, and she knew he would be there, waiting to reclaim his property.

That was all she had become, the property of a man who set store by what his money could achieve for him. He had patiently watched her father ruin himself, and then he had stepped in and taken over what remained of the St Cyr estate . . . Cathlamet and herself.

Bliss stared resentfully at her reflection in the mirror, sweeping her desperate eyes up and down her own figure. That was all Paris Apollonaris wanted of her! He didn't care two hoots on a tin flute that inside her skin she was pulsing with her own wants.

Damn him! She flung away from the mirror and hurried out of the powder-room, and instantly she saw his tall figure awaiting her in the foyer, her lynx jacket ready for her to slip into.

Outside the restaurant the night air was curiously soft and the sky was alight with stars. He paused on the pavement beside the car and took a deep breath of the air which held the promise of summertime. 'I grow to like your country, Bliss, it has a lot to offer.'

'And you're busy taking your share, aren't you?' she said coldly.

He brought his gaze down from the stars to her face, and then with a frown he flung open the door beside her. 'Get in,' he said curtly. She did so, withdrawn into her seat so that when he entered she wouldn't have to feel herself near to him. They swept away from the Ruby Tower and after several minutes Bliss realised that he wasn't heading for Earls Court but for the very centre of London. Where were they going now? Not to some nightclub, she hoped. The last thing she wanted was to be in his arms, dancing with him.

He pulled into a side turning just off Piccadilly Circus and drew into the kerb. 'I fancy a stroll,' he informed her. 'Come along.'

Bliss didn't argue with him; a stroll was preferable to a nightclub and though it was late there were numerous people still about, drawn to the lights of Piccadilly, blazing in the shopfronts, in the arcades and at the front of the theatres and cinemas.

Paris took her hand and slipped it through the crook of his arm holding it there in case she thwarted him. 'Listen to the birds,' he said, for as they strolled along high above them was the restless cheeping and cooing of the thousands of birds who had adapted to a strange pattern of life because it gave them sustenance. Up there on the rooftops of the buildings they roosted, kept active and awake by the many bright lights of the city centre.

Bliss listened in a kind of wonderment, for the rooftops were as alive with birds as the cliffs of some seaside resort. 'You see,' Paris murmured, 'it's possible to adapt to a situation without breaking your heart.'

'Possibly,' she said, 'but it somehow makes me sad to hear those birds, restless and sleepless, when deep in the country their cousins are peacefully at roost. It doesn't seem natural.'

'It isn't,' he agreed. 'But life in the city provides them with their bread, so don't feel too saddened. Many generations of them have lived out their lives on the rooftops of Piccadilly; they have known no other way of life and so it isn't strange to them. But in your two years in London you have often felt a stranger, have you not?'

'Sometimes,' she admitted, 'but I'm adapting.'

'No,' he disagreed. 'I suspect that you never stop thinking of Cathlamet, there on the border of the moors where you rode your ponies when you were a child. Cathlamet is waiting for your return.'

Her heart turned over when he said that . . . so that was why he had brought her to the Circus to listen to the midnight birds, so he could arouse her nostalgia for the house in which generations of her family had lived . . . and loved.

'As you told me,' her voice had cooled again, 'you never do anything from motives of sentiment.'

He didn't reply, with his dark head tilted back he listened to the midnight birds. There was on his face, she saw, a look bordering on the sadness she felt for those restless creatures, twittering and flapping their wings in the dazzle of lights that kept night at bay.

She gave a little shiver and he noticed. 'Time to go home,' he said, and they retraced their steps to the car. Soon it was warm inside and Bliss felt a slight easing of her tension.

'I—I suppose you'll start making arrangements,' she said tentatively.

'For our wedding, eh?'

'Yes—I hope you don't intend it to be a big affair?'

'Neither of us want that.' He spoke decisively. 'We shall be married in Athens and then we shall set sail for Dovima, an island I own in the Aegean. We shall honeymoon on the island.'

'I see.' Bliss felt an intense awareness of him when he spoke that word which for couples in love must be an exciting one, implying sweetness and romance. 'I suppose I'm not to have any say in anything?'

'You may choose your own dress,' he said drily.

'Are we being married in a church?'

'Of course.'

'Will it please your mother that you're marrying an English girl?'

'Not entirely.'

'Oh, Paris—please——' Bliss's voice broke on a note of pleading. 'How could we ever be happy——?'

'Happiness is something I've never thought a lot about.' The car slid smoothly into the kerb in front of the house where Bliss lived and the moment it came to a standstill she released herself from the seat-belt, clicked open the door and fled up the front steps of the house. She was fumbling in her bag for her key when Paris swung her to face him, his strong arms fully enveloping her. She gazed up at him wildly, the light beside the door shining on her face and revealing her distress.

'You think only of yourself,' she gasped. 'What if I hope to find a little happiness—doesn't that count?'

'You don't believe that you can be happy with me?' he asked.

'With you?' She looked incredulous that he should even ask. 'I'm your bargain bride, remember? I'm bought and paid for!'

'Yes, so you are.' He thrust his fingers through her hair, then holding her by her nape he kissed her with total possessiveness, a man who all his life had been a stranger to tenderness. Bliss submitted to him because there seemed no way of fighting him, but she didn't respond to the demanding warmth of his mouth. She accepted his kisses with a deliberate passiveness, and with a muttered Greek oath he abruptly released her.

'I'll melt you,' he warned, his eyes dangerously agleam in his dark face.

'When ice melts, Paris, all that's left is a puddle of water.' Head tilted back, she defied his dangerous eyes.

'You always have an answer, don't you?' His

mouth gave a sardonic twist. 'Go to your bed, *pedhi mou*. I shall be in touch.' He took her hand and laid his lips where her ring rested, then he turned on his heel, ran down the steps and strode to the Jaguar. He was, Bliss told herself, as flexible of body and as intent on his prey as some great jungle cat, and it also seemed to her that he could be as cruel when it suited his purpose.

She went indoors and closed the door on the sound of his car driving away, heading for his apartment above the Club Cassandra, where weak men such as her father and Justin fell victim to the shrewdness of men such as Paris Apollonaris.

What would he do, she wondered, if she refused to come to heel when he called?

Oh God, she knew the answer ... he would make Justin suffer the ignominy of being brought back to England under arrest!

The decision was made for her; she knew that she must marry Paris and keep the St Cyr escutcheon from being blotted by her brother who was more reckless than truly criminal.

Right now he was on the high seas, probably gambling away his pocket money in the ship's casino, while here she was trudging dispiritedly up a flight of stairs that creaked with age, to a landing redolent of boiled cabbage, to a pair of rooms that were, at the very least, her private domain.

She glanced around her, knowing that in the very near future she would be saying *adieu* to Earls Court in order to fly off to Athens to be joined in rather unholy wedlock to a man who had never voiced those time-honoured words ... I love you.

CHAPTER SIX

THE very perfection of her wedding dress made Bliss all the sadder, for it was the kind of gown which a bride should be happy and eager to be married in.

It wasn't a traditional bridal gown which swept the floor and had a trailing veil attached, but was of magnolia lace over a satin underslip, mid-calf length and with a heart-shaped bodice that showed off the slender length of Bliss's neck. Without putting up an argument she had gone obediently to the couturier in South Moulton Street to which Paris had sent her, where the arrangements had already been made for her fittings . . . not only for the wedding dress but for the remainder of her trousseau.

She had submitted because trying to argue with Paris was like trying to climb a slippery pole, there was just no way of holding on to her resolves where he was concerned. Not only was he Greek and entrenched in the idea that a man was head of the house, but he had a natural gift for command, and he had commanded the very best of apparel for the girl he was going to marry.

Bliss fixed to her hair the little lace cap that went with her dress, then she opened the white hide box which had been delivered to the door of her hotel room an hour ago. There on satin lay a double strand of stunning pearls, the ruby clasp gleaming deep red beside the glossy pallor of the pearls. She clasped them about her neck, for there had been a little white card with them on which Paris had written: *Let the pearls be your tears and save your smiles for me. And don't mind when you look from your window and see rain on the rooftops. Here in my country we believe that rain on a wedding day brings luck and fertility.*

The implications in that final word made Bliss grip the strands of pearls so nervously that they might have broken had they not been strung on very strong silk.

She moved her gaze up and down her reflection in the mirror, hearing the sound of the rain as it beat against the windows of this hotel that faced the Hill of Mars, where the Apostle Paul had preached the loving goodness of a God who neither lived in a temple nor wreaked vengeance when His will was crossed.

The sound of the rain reminded her vividly of the evening when she had gone to Paris at the Club Cassandra and pleaded with him not to wreak vengeance on her brother ... instead he had turned his sword against her, and putting a hand to her side Bliss felt a kind of ache which had been with her for days.

It was the kind of ache that sometimes reached into her throat so that she wanted to cry in order to relieve it. It was nerves, fear, resentment, all mixed up together, and with each beat of her heart, each tick of the watch on her wrist, the time drew near for the wedding car to come for her.

She and Paris had arrived in Athens the evening before, and all she had seen of the city was the floodlit Parthenon from the window of the cab which had driven them into the city from the airport.

'Won't it seem strange to your mother—to your friends, that they don't know me? That they've never met me?' Bliss had asked, in another desperate effort to postpone the wedding.

Paris had shaken his head. 'In Greece it's accepted that strangers marry. For my mother and friends it's sufficient that I am marrying. I think they had rather given up hope that I would.'

'Oh—why?' She had felt momentarily curious about this aspect of his life; she didn't doubt that there had been women in his life, for he was so entirely male, but it did seem surprising that he hadn't married, in view of his financial success and that need in the Greek to have a son to follow him and carry on his name.

'Because I have no sisters,' Paris replied. 'In Greece it's a matter of family pride and honour that a brother, if he has sisters, should see them settled in homes of their own before he looks around for a likely wife. Even today many of my countrymen still do this; they work extremely hard to provide sisters with the dowrie that will attract a suitor, and then they find themselves hard up so they need to seek a wife with a dowry. In village areas the dowry can take the form of a flock of sheep or goats and maybe a couple of good horses, but in the cities gold pounds are preferred.'

'The marriage market place,' Bliss had said bitterly. 'If you hadn't been rich yourself, then I'd have been no good for you—you know I haven't a dowry.'

'No?' He had sat there in his corner of the cab and she had seen his eyes glittering. 'As you say, I'm a rich enough Greek to be able to pick and choose. Doubtless many of our customs will seem strange to you, and even I, a Greek, am appalled that in too many of our villages the ill-educated, black-clad matrons are the ones who condemn modern ways, and who make life a misery for those women who have fallen from grace, causing them to become outcasts. Yes, I am rich now, *moiya*, and I can afford to wear fine suits, to eat good food, to own houses, and marry the girl of my choice. Nonetheless I don't forget my beginnings.'

The glitter of his eyes had held Bliss as she listened to him, there in the cab that sped along the dual carriageway that led into the city, towards Constitution Square.

'T—t!' Paris made that exclamation that was so purely Greek, and so significant of his feelings when he spoke of his early years. 'I don't forget the small boy who was never allowed to join in the games of the other children because I was an outcast along with my mother, made so by the spiteful tongues of those old women who sat at their doors and kept a beady eye on younger women. Sometimes other boys would throw stones at me, and the girls would chant the name for my sort of child, heard in the kitchens of their parents. When they called me by that name I would kick the dirt and square my chin and vow to myself that one day—one day I would return to Greece to be married to a girl other men would envy.'

He had laughed in that grating way of his; a

laugh dipped in the bitter wine of his memories.
'I have such a girl in you, Bliss, and tomorrow in
front of a congregation you will become mine.'

Now in her hotel bedroom Bliss stared at her
reflection in the mirror and saw the look in her
own eyes, not one of expectation and eagerness
but one which any trapped creature would have
in its eyes, a kind of pain and doom.

She gave a start when she heard someone
knocking on the door of the outer room. She braced
herself and went to slide the bolt. When she opened
the door she found a woman standing there, some
years older than herself, undoubtedly Greek, and
clad in a blue silk suit and a rather pretty straw hat
with little flowers tucked into the brim.

'Hello,' she said in English, her attractively
impish face breaking into a smile. 'I am Kara
Savidge, a friend of your fiancé's. My husband
and I have come to take you to the Chuch of St
Nikolaos.'

'Oh——' Bliss fell back a step, for the advent
of the young Greek woman was quite unexpected.
Paris hadn't mentioned her by name; all he had
said was that just before eleven o'clock this
morning she would be taken by car to the church.

Kara Savidge glanced at her wristwatch. 'We
have a few minutes to spare, so may I come in
and speak with you? No doubt you are feeling
nervous at the prospect of being married in a
Greek church – in fact you do look rather pale.'

'Yes, do come in.' Bliss pulled the door a little
wider so the young Greek woman could enter the
sitting-room.

'My husband Lucan is waiting for us down in

the lobby,' Kara explained, her smile a singularly nice one. 'Lucan is of Irish descent, but I can see that you are purely English. You have beautiful hair, *thespinis*, and because in certain ways Paris reminds me of my brother I'm unsurprised that he is taking a wife of your fair appearance. My brother Paul married an English girl . . . some Greek men are strongly attracted to fair women.'

'My kind of hair isn't easily manageable.' Bliss gave a strained smile. 'I envy Greek women like yourself who have naturally wavy hair.'

Kara Savidge was very dark-haired, and in the lobes of her ears she wore small golden rings. She wasn't exactly pretty, Bliss thought, but she had something bewitching about her; in her large dark eyes there lay a deep and genuine concern for anyone who seemed in trouble.

'It really is just like Paris to bring you straight to Athens and not give you time to adjust to the climate and the customs.' Kara laid a gentle hand on Bliss's arm. 'These Greek men, eh? In public so haughty and distant, while in private they are so passionate. How they can hate, and how they can adore! But not always do they fully understand the needs of women, or even assume that women should have needs different from their own. I know, *thespinis*, that the love of a Greek can be a kind of captivity, for as I say, Paris is cut from the same kind of cloth as my brother.'

When Kara Savidge spoke of passion and captivity Bliss could feel her nerves like needle-points pressing her flesh. Those were indeed the words that described Paris's attitude towards her . . . she was the captive of his loveless passion.

As if reading something of this in Bliss's eyes, Kara said quietly: 'I suppose you've not met Paris's mother, not if this is your first trip to Greece?'

Bliss shook her head and unaware she was playing nervously with the ruby ring on her left hand. 'Paris has talked about her, but he's her son and we—we naturally think kindly of our parents. Do you know her, Kara?'

'Yes. Lucan and I met her once when we were invited for a holiday on Dovima, the island which Paris bought for himself.'

'What sort of person is she?' Bliss tried to speak composedly, but she was beginning to form a mental picture of a possessive and rather hard-natured woman who would resent her because she wasn't Greek like Paris. 'Did you—like her?'

'I admired her,' Kara replied. 'Life didn't treat her very well until Paris started to be a successful man and could give her all the things she never had. She lives on the island, but not in the main villa. Paris has undoubtedly told you that he had the two houses built when he became owner of Dovima?'

Bliss shook her head. 'He hasn't talked a lot about the island—all I really know is that we're going to—to spend our honeymoon there.'

'I think you'll like it.' Kara smiled reassuringly. 'All that was on it when Paris took it over was the remains of an old Venetian castle, a kind of look-out used long ago so that if pirate ships were sighted, warning fires could be lit on the hillside and the cannons could be fired from the walls. Those strong old Venetian walls now surround the villa itself, for Paris had the house built inside them, the remainder of the ruins being used for rock gardens and pathways. You can see carved into the walls the Lion of St Mark, which Lucan always says is a good enough escutcheon for Paris himself.'

'Really?' Bliss gave a brief smile. 'Why do you suppose your husband says that?'

'First because he's still very Irish, despite the fact that he was born in the West Indies, and secondly because he calls Paris a lion-hearted man—Paris, as you know, has had to fight every inch of the way to get where he is today. He started out with nothing but his brain and his sinews, and now he has—a girl like you.'

'Me?' Bliss said winsomely. 'I'm scared stiff that his mother is going to disapprove of me because I'm not Greek.'

'It's true that Greeks are very insular when it comes to marriage,' Kara admitted. 'But if you love him, then you'll win her over.'

Bliss's heart seemed to trip on itself at the word love, and to hide what might have leapt into her eyes she glanced at her wristwatch. 'The time's getting on, should we be going?'

'Yes.' Kara came to Bliss and took her by the hands. 'Don't worry too much—a Greek wedding is far less formal than your own British kind. People will come in from the street when they know a wedding is taking place, and the bride and groom aren't alone at the altar table because the guests are allowed to stand close to them in order to be witness to the ceremony. It's rather like a party.'

'Paris said it would be a quiet affair—how many guests are there going to be?'

'About two dozen.' Kara squeezed her hands. 'You have to realise that Paris has personal and business friends in Athens and they expect to see him married—it's a matter of *philotimo*, a very Greek word which combines pride and honour out in the open for others to admire. Having *philotimo* is important to a Greek, as it's important to him that the girl he weds should be chaste. What of your own family and friends?'

'My only brother is travelling abroad.' Bliss felt the warmth of Kara's slim hands against the coolness of her own skin. 'I have a few friends in London, but they work for their living and couldn't be expected to be at my wedding in Athens of all places.'

'Which makes it rather lonely for you,' Kara said understandingly. 'Then I'm pleased that Lucan and I can be with you; I think you'll like my husband. Now let me take a look at you to make sure all is in order.'

She scanned Bliss from head to toe and nodded her approval. 'Your dress is lovely, and the simplicity of the style suits you, just as that magnolia colour sets off your hair. And such splendid pearls!'

'A gift from Paris.' Bliss ran her hand down their silkiness. 'In England we have a superstition that pearls bring bad luck.'

'Hush, you mustn't speak of bad luck on your wedding day!'

Bliss watched as Kara crossed herself, still so Greek even though she wasn't married to one.

'Are you going to carry flowers?' Kara asked, glancing around for them.

'Orchids,' said Bliss. 'Paris has arranged that they be kept in refrigeration here at the hotel, and I'm to ask for them at the desk. All this—oh, it's so strange! In England the bouquet is delivered the morning of the wedding, along with a tray of carnations for the guests. There are bridesmaids scampering about in their finery, perhaps music playing on the radio, and sandwiches and coffee being made.' She drew a shaky sigh. 'I—I can hardly believe that in half an hour I'm going to be married!'

'Once you are in church with Paris you will feel more at ease. Come,' Kara drew her to the door, 'let us go down to Lucan.'

Bliss could feel a tremor in her legs as she and Kara made their way to the lift. She'd had a cup of coffee but hadn't managed to eat more than half a *brioche*, and she told herself that it was being a little famished that made her feel so cold and empty. Pray God she didn't faint at the altar table, not with two dozen Greek friends of Paris's looking on—what a fool they'd assume her to be, fainting for marrying a man who had wealth and power, and *philotimo*.

Was Paris really proud of what he had accomplished in getting her to Athens to be his bride bought with the money which had slid through her brother's fingers like golden water?

Down in the hotel lobby she was introduced to Kara's tall and striking husband, who ceased his prowling as they came into view, striding towards them and fixing Bliss with grey eyes with a green fire flickering in them, set in a sun-browned face beneath thick hair the colour of a fox's pelt.

Not handsome but certainly noticeable. Probably not always gentle but certainly a gentleman.

'There the two of you are,' he said in a deep voice. 'I began to think you were going to gossip the day away.'

Introductions took place, then Kara said to him: 'Darling, go to the desk and ask the clerk for the wedding bouquet, which is being kept in refrigeration.'

He slowly raised an eyebrow that matched his hair. 'I hope, Bliss, that it's only your bouquet that's going to be nice and cool at this wedding— is it?'

Then he strode over to the reception desk, while Kara gave a little laugh. 'Lucan has a rather sardonic sense of humour, which is why he gets along with Paris, but at the same time he has a vein of Irish mysticism in him. I love him with my soul, but there's no way to stop him speaking his mind—you have warmth in your heart for Paris, haven't you?'

There in the lobby the two women stood looking at each other, and suddenly a flicker of pain went across Kara's face. 'I knew it! Paris, like my brother Paul, has searched for his Helen and made for himself a private battle of Troy, is that not so?'

'I'm afraid so,' Bliss said, very quietly.

Lucan returned with the bouquet, uncaring that people glanced at him with a certain amusement. Bliss took from him the exquisite pale orchids just faintly tipped at their rims with rose-madder; satin ribbons. hung from them, fluttering in the rainy wind as she stepped into the street with Kara and Lucan, the three of them hastening into the limousine that was to take them to the Church of St Nikolaos.

This was it, Bliss told herself, still feeling cold even though she wore the lovely pale mink coat which Paris had bought her. She held the orchids carefully in her hands, listening to the deep timbre of Lucan Savidge's voice as he talked of the island where he and Kara lived with their twin sons, left at home in the care of their West Indian nanny while he and Kara attended Paris's wedding.

'How did you come to meet Paris?' Bliss found herself asking.

'Some years ago, when my plantation was in ruins, I needed a backer so I could start to rebuild. I could have asked my brother-in-law for assistance, but I preferred to keep the matter impersonal. I approached Elias Mercantile and became acquainted with Paris, who backed me all the way, even though there was still a good chance that he'd lose his money. He didn't, and now Dragon Bay flourishes and my boys' heritage is secure, thanks to a man who never had a penny to call his own when he was a boy!'

Bliss could feel those grey-green eyes upon her profile as Lucan spoke those words ... did he suspect that Paris had bought her, a toy to ease the memory of a toyless childhood?

'I'm glad for you and Kara,' she said, wishing sadly that she could feel glad as the car approached the white-walled, blue-domed church, with rounded windows of stained glass.

Her heart beat rapidly . . . in a very short time she would be committed to Paris Apollonaris for better, for worse. As the deep-toned bells began their clangour, Bliss accepted her fate.

CHAPTER SEVEN

INSIDE the doorway of the church Paris waited with a woman who Bliss knew right away was his mother. She was fairly tall, with a fine, work-worn face which retained some of the striking beauty it must have had when she was young. Her eyes didn't pierce Bliss, as she had expected; they were slumbrously dark, rather sad, and they dwelt on Bliss as she entered in her pale lace dress, having removed her mink coat and left it in the bridal car. She wasn't wet from the rain, for she had been met at the car door by an attendant holding open a large umbrella.

Upon coming face to face with her bride-groom's mother Bliss didn't know whether to smile or not. She felt a strange, unreal sensation, almost as if she were dreaming, and even when Paris spoke to her, his voice didn't dispel her sense of dreaming.

'Let me introduce you to my mother; only moments ago she remarked that if I had to marry a foreign girl, then she hoped I had chosen a charming one.' He shared his rather grave smile between the two women who in a little while would be his only kin, one of them dressed in the lacy glamour of a wedding gown, the other clad in a sober black dress, grey-streaked black hair drawn back in a nape-knot, drops of jet suspended in her earlobes.

No two women could have been more of a contrast; they were like sunlight and shadow at either side of the man.

Then with an abrupt touch of shyness Magda Apollonaris stepped towards Bliss, took hold of her face and kissed her on either cheek.

'Make happy my son,' she said in broken English.

'I—I shall try,' Bliss replied. She didn't dare to look at Paris, and a moment later they were walking arm in arm to the altar table, and Bliss was aware in a dreamlike way of people watching them, dark eyes gleaming in warm-skinned faces through a cool duskiness where gold and silver ikons caught the light of the many candles.

Bliss smelled the candle smoke and the drift of incense and also the carnations in the lapels of the men who were present. She was aware of Paris's mother standing behind them, the best man beside her, clad soberly like Paris, who was very upright and very dark beside Bliss's fair slenderness.

The remainder of the guests clustered around the bridal group and the priest began to chant the phrases of the marriage service, which truly was Greek so far as Bliss was concerned. Paris had told her on the plane journey to Athens that during the course of the ceremony the priest would intone: 'Woman must fear man,' and when he did so, Paris would give her a little nod which was her cue to tread on his foot, a subtle Greek joke, which would cause amusement among the guests.

Came the moment, when with a slight

movement of his dark head Paris indicated that she place her foot on his. She obeyed, and instantly a ripple of laughter ran round the church. It lightened Bliss's heart a little, but she knew how deadly cold was her hand when the gold marriage rings were exchanged three times before the rings were finally placed on their right hands, there to remain if fate decreed.

It had rather surprised her that the Greek church didn't frown on divorce but accepted that as many of it's country's marriages were arranged there was no guarantee that husband and wife would fall in love. A Greek, in fact, was permitted to marry three times if he so wished.

The wedding coronets were produced, these being fashioned from fine leather to imitate twigs and buds, and joined by a fine length of ribbon. The best man held them overhead as the final rites of the marriage were intoned, and as with the rings the coronets were exchanged three times before bride and groom were led round the altar table by the priest, this procedure being called the wedding dance.

During this ritual the guests aimed rice and rose petals and sweet almonds, and Bliss began to understand why Paris had said that a Greek marriage was less formal than an English one.

With rose petals clinging to her lace and rice grains down the neck of her dress, and a slight bubble of hysteria inside her, Bliss took sips of the wedding wine from the priest, then a big silver Bible was held so she and Paris could kiss it.

They were married, and in a daze she walked

with her arm through the crook of his, to the door of
the church where the guests crowded around them,
hugging, kissing, offering good wishes, some of
them wiping off a sentimental tear as bride and
groom ran through the rain to the car, which was
taking them directly to the harbour where Paris had
his caique waiting for them.

As they sped through Athens to the harbour of
Piraeus Paris drew the soft fur of her coat around
Bliss's shoulders and instantly she sensed in his
touch his new possessiveness. 'You looked
charming,' he said.

'I hope your friends were suitably impressed.'
She enveloped herself in the huge collar of the
coat, remembering how at the door of the church
he had given their wedding coronets to his
mother, who had held them close to her as if they
consoled her.

'My mother liked you,' he murmured.

'I—I liked her,' Bliss rejoined, for it had been a
relief to find his mother so reclusive instead of
dominating and jealous, as the mother of an only
son might well be on the day he took a wife.

'Can't you share a little of the liking with me?'
He spoke drily. 'I am my mother's son, and you
saw the kind of woman she is.'

Bliss gave him a noncommittal look, allowing
him to take her right hand into his so he could
admire the glistening gold band on it. 'When our
guests join us for our reception on the caique do
try and look as if you are a bride instead of a
mourner.'

'You know I didn't want the fuss and bother of
a reception——'

'Come, it would be ungracious on our wedding day not to share cake and champagne with our well-wishers. Be a reasonable child!'

'Always my wishes are childish,' she retorted. 'Always your word is law!'

He squeezed her fingers and didn't deny her accusation.

'Are you afraid,' she asked, 'that your friends will guess that I'm your bride under duress?'

'I'd prefer them to think, if only for my mother's sake, that you like being my wife—I'm not so unnatural that I enjoy being thought of as a man who has you against your will.'

'Are you really suggesting that you can be hurt by me?' Bliss smiled at the thought. 'I was really beginning to think that there was no chink in your armour.'

'There is a chink where my mother is concerned.' His face hardened. 'Hurt her in any way and you'll suffer for it, so let that be a warning.'

Bliss lowered her gaze, hating the way he could make her feel afraid when his face went like stone, and his eyes seethed with the many angers of a man who had endured along with his mother the insults and the hungers of never being asked to share the fireside of a neighbour. That proud woman had struggled alone to feed and clothe her son, and now it was his turn to ensure that she never went cold and hungry ever again.

Kara Savidge had mentioned the passion that Greeks could feel, and Bliss felt in her husband a passionate protectiveness where his mother was concerned.

'It would never occur to me to hurt your mother,' she assured him. 'She didn't have to show me any kindness today, but she did. I'm the stranger who has married her son and she didn't have to—to accept me.'

'She accepts you on my behalf. I am all she has and you are now a part of me, like one of my arms.' There was iron in his voice when he said this, and iron in his grip when he took her by the chin and forced her to look at him. 'A Greek doesn't ask a woman to fear him, but he does expect her to realise that she belongs to him once they become man and wife. You belong to me, Bliss. Every hair of you is mine; every inch of white skin, every little bead of sweat and every tear in your eyes. I say this not because of the money; I say it because it is so!'

Slowly he moved her hand to his mouth and she felt the warm pressure of his lips on her skin.

'There are,' he murmured, 'countless pebbles on a beach, and many of them are attractive. A man spends part of his life treating the world like a beach and women like pebbles which he feels impelled to pick up, to fondle for a while, and then discard. Then all at once there is a certain pebble which he cannot allow to slip through his fingers, and so he decides to keep it in his possession. You are my possession, and I say to hell with the silly, sentimental avowals that too many people make and too many people break.'

'Avowals aren't the only things that people break,' Bliss reminded him.

'Hearts, my dear?' He looked sardonic even as he pressed her hand against his hard-boned

cheek, shaved smooth that morning without soap
or water in order, in the Greek tradition, to prove
his manhood. 'Do you truly believe, *moiya*, that
the heart is the seat of the passions?'

She flushed at the smile that kindled in his
eyes. 'I—I was talking about love——'

'Love?' He arched a black eyebrow. 'Now there
is a provocative word and I wonder what you
mean by it?'

'You know full well what I mean.' Bliss jerked
her chin and instantly his hand slid down to
enclose her neck, which was more sensitive to his
touch, more vulnerable in its soft slenderness to
the deliberate caress of his fingers; the lean but
hardened fingers of a man who has worked with
them for years: back-breaking work of the kind
she couldn't even imagine and which would have
crippled someone like Justin.

In all fairness she understood what motivated
him in relation to herself, but he seemed not to
care that she shrank from belonging to him
without any love.

'I grant that our relationship wouldn't be good
material for a romantic story,' he drawled. 'All I
can offer you in the way of romance is our sailing
by caique to Dovima; it's a pity about the rain,
but it may ease off this afternoon and you'll see
the beauty of the Aegean, the sea of islands,
where some men sail and never return home.
When the sun sets across the Aegean it's as if it
strikes gold in the sea. You'll be enthralled,
moiya.'

But even as he spoke Bliss could feel herself
shrinking inwardly from his forty-four-inch chest

and the bronzed skin of his hands and face. The very look of him was a living, breathing threat . . . unlike other people, they hadn't come face to face in mutual desire; he had her in exchange for money and she felt cheapened by the entire transaction.

'Our story would make good material for *Private Eye*,' she said coldly.

'T—t! I give to you what I can!' His nostrils flared. 'It isn't in my nature to regard a woman as some kind of shrine where I'm supposed to worship!'

'I never supposed it was, Paris.'

'But is it what you expect?' In anger, in the gloom of the car, his dark-skinned face was almost ferocious, his eyes burning her with their raw gold.

'Hardly.' She gave a slight shrug.

'Then what in the name of the devil are we talking about, a groom and his bride on their way to the wedding breakfast? Look at you, you are wearing mink and pearls, and your husband is a man with an island of his own and the respect of people such as the Savidges and the brother of Kara who is the head of the Stephanous shipping line. I am not a nobody! Is that what you are thinking, that you have lowered your status in marrying me?'

'No——'

His hand gripped her throat as if he felt like throttling her, but when she made no sound and just looked at him as if willing him to give into his anger, he slackened his grip and pushed her away from him.

'We Greeks are proud, but you take the prize, my child. Ah well, as we say in Greece, chastity is the prize reserved for a loveless match, and you have that to give me even if you haven't anything else.'

'You seem so sure about that, Paris.' Nothing short of torture would have stopped Bliss from saying those words to him, with the forlorn hope that she might plant a seed of doubt in his mind.

'I am sure,' he said arrogantly.

'You probably would be sure if I were a Greek girl,' Bliss rejoined. 'But I'm English, and we now regard it as rather turn-of-the-century to expect women to be pure as driven snow while men enjoy their fling before marrying. That double standard has long fallen from its pole in my country.'

'I daresay it has, Bliss, and no doubt many English women enjoy what you call a fling, but I don't have to be clairvoyant in order to read your character. You're fastidious, my child. It's that in you that makes you hate me for making you marry me. You are the type of girl who still likes to believe in the knight on a white charger, glistening with silver armour and a picture of gallantry.'

'You make me sound a naïve fool,' she protested.

'No,' he shook his head, 'an idealistic one.'

She didn't argue with him, for up to a point he was right about her. That she was fastidious was in the tapering grace of her cheekbones, and in the translucent grey of her eyes as she sat there,

her face half hidden in the big mink collar of the
champagne-coloured coat.

In some secret compartment of her mind she
wished that Justin could be like him, so
successful, so tough-fibred, so innately trust-
worthy when it came to business.

'You are the most unguarded girl I've ever
met,' Paris told her. 'You are rather like snow
that a man's foot could trample and spoil!' His
gaze upon her seemed to penetrate to the depths
of her eyes. 'That we are here together is the way
it must be!'

'You tell yourself that, Paris, in order to ease
your sense of guilt.'

'My guilt?' he exclaimed.

'Yes, because you're Greek and you like to
think that you have *philotimo*.'

His eyes narrowed to slits of gold ... a
glowering gold through the darkness of his
lashes. 'Be careful what you say when you speak
to me of *philotimo*,' he warned. 'You're treading
on dangerous ground, Bliss.'

'I've been on dangerous ground ever since I
met you, Paris. I stepped upon the quicksands
the day you were at Cathlamet in order to accept
the deeds of the estate from my father. I didn't
know that until he died and the solicitor spoke of
it to Justin and myself, but when I recollected
your devil-darkness and the swift way you drove
away in your Jaguar I felt unsurprised that you
had some hold upon us. You were unlike anyone
else I'd ever seen at Cathlamet. You weren't a
horseman in breeches and boots, or one of the
bluff Yorkshiremen my father liked to drink with.

I should have guessed that day that you were going to cast your dark shadow over my life.'

'Heaven stay my hand!' Paris muttered through his teeth. 'I didn't ruin your father, he was self-destructive and he ruined himself. I picked up the pieces of your life that he had scattered across the card tables. T—t, we have spoken of this before and it begins to grate on me. You are spoiling our wedding day!'

'Good,' she retorted. 'Hearing you say that is the only thing I've enjoyed today.'

'*Efharisto*.' He sarcastically thanked her in Greek. 'You are asking to be taught a lesson when we find ourselves alone on Dovima.'

'But your mother will be there——'

'My mother remains in Athens with a friend during the two weeks of our honeymoon.'

'I see.' Bliss felt her heart give a thump as she realised what it was going to mean being alone with Paris . . . she looked at his shoulders clothed in the fine dark cloth and they threatened her. She looked at his hands that were so alive and strong, a gleam of gold on the right one that proclaimed his right to run those hands over her body.

She looked into his eyes and knew that he was reading her mind as if her thoughts were written across her brow.

'Yes,' he murmured, 'we shall be all alone except for the few people who run the villa for me and care for the gardens. We have no neighbours except a few goats and the dolphins that swim offshore. Brace yourself for what is to come, my darling.'

And he didn't say it coldly, he slurred the words with a deliberate sensuality, leaning towards her with his nostrils tensed as if to catch the scent of her skin and hair. She felt his dark power encompassing her, and a kind of helplessness seemed to hold her in its spell when he took her face between his hands and placed kisses against her eyes, each one in turn, until lingeringly he moved his lips to her mouth.

When at last he drew a little away from her Bliss gazed into his eyes and saw tiny reflections of herself in the dark pupils, widened by his sensual mood.

She was apathetic, for there was nothing profound in his feeling for her; it was entirely physical. That ceremony in the church with its glowing colours and its incense had not been the culmination of their romantic dreams. A sigh slid from her lips and brushed his.

Instantly his eyes narrowed and her tiny reflected self was hidden away behind his black lashes. 'Think yourself fortunate,' he told her, 'that I have a streak of relentless patience often lacking in my fellow Greeks. From where it comes the devil knows, but be grateful for it—any other man might take you by the shoulders and shake you for the rag-doll that you become when you are kissed. Kisses, *moiya*, are only the prelude to passion.'

'Passion!' She looked scornful. 'That's all I am where you're concerned, an object of your passions!'

'Quite.' He bit out the word. 'Right now you're brave with your insults—but don't forget what a vengeful man I am.'

'I know exactly what sort of man you are,' Bliss said defiantly. 'You have what every successful self-made man has, nerves of steel and feelings to match!'

'I also have some of the East in my veins, inherited from my mother, and I don't take insolence from a woman—least of all from my wife!'

Those words struck through Bliss, they were so possessive, reminding her vividly of those words in church: 'Woman must fear man!'

'You can't stop me from speaking my mind,' she retorted, 'unless you plan to cut out my tongue—I believe it was done long ago to women in the *seraglio*, who were then thrown into the Bosphorous.'

'Doubtless.' He gave a short laugh. 'What a very vivid imagination you have, my dear child— no wonder that brother of yours was able to convince you that I had designs on your virtue!'

Paris leaned back in his seat and in the silence which followed his remark the rain drummed upon the roof of the limousine.

'Because of you, Madame Apollonaris, I never had any intention of having your brother taken into custody—what purpose would it have served except to hurt you?' He quirked an eyebrow. 'But you came to my club believing his story, that in exchange for you I would let him off the hook. You accused me of setting a trap for him when all I did was to provide him with the only job he's capable of, being among gamblers who enjoy the smooth style that Justin exudes.

'My dear naïve one, I never intended to take

you in exchange for his freedom from justice, but
he convinced you of it. I laid no traps for either
of you—you offered yourself in your innocence,
and I was never a Greek to refuse a gift from the
gods. You are very attractive, my child, and I am
tired of being lonely. You will do for me even if
you don't love me.'

He snapped his fingers, hard and dismissively.
'So much for love. Love is an enigma!'

'Do you mean,' Bliss gazed at him incredulously, 'that I could have walked out of the Club
Cassandra a free person, unbound by—by any
obligation to you?'

Paris inclined his head and the look in his eyes
was purely sardonic.

'I—I could have gone home that night and
telephoned Justin to tell him he had nothing to
fear?' Her heart was beating with thumps that
made her speak breathlessly.

'Exactly.'

'But you let me believe otherwise—that you
intended a reprisal unless I married you?'

'Yes.' He confessed quite shamelessly, and
Bliss felt driven to an act that would relieve the
tension that gripped her by the roots of her hair.
She wrenched off her wedding ring and flung it
at him, seeing the gold circlet strike his shoulder
and fall into the crook of his arm, where he
retrieved it.

'Y-you know what you can do with that,' she
snapped furiously. 'I never wanted to marry you,
a-and I won't stay married to you!'

'You will, my dear.' Suddenly his eyes held a
rather deadly glint. 'You won't make a fool of me

in front of our guests—do that and I shall immediately cable the ship on which your brother travels and inform the Captain that he has on board a thief who must be put under arrest.'

'You wouldn't——' Even as Bliss spoke the words she knew them to be superfluous, for his face was as if chiselled from stone and his eyes were the cold amber of a lion confronting its prey.

'Try me,' he said, his voice equally stony. 'Walk away from me when we reach the harbour and find out for yourself that your precious brother has been locked up. This time, Bliss, I mean every word I say. This time we aren't playing games. You have married me, and I don't intend to let a slip of a girl walk out on me, and I know you won't for Justin's sake.'

'You're bluffing, Paris!'

He shook his head. 'Not any more, *pedhi mou*. When you came to me at the Club Cassandra you were Bliss St Cyr. Right now you are Madame Apollonaris; and if you value your brother's skin—and I know you do—you will go on board the *Stella Maris* with me and you will smile at my friends like a dutiful bride. Understood?'

And as he said this he reached for her right hand and replaced the gold ring which had now assumed for Bliss the proportions of a handcuff. Her cold hand trembled with nerves ... her entire body was vibrating to the thump of her heart.

'You damned devil,' she muttered.

He shrugged his shoulders. 'That's what you assumed at the Club Cassandra and that's why you are with me right now. Paint someone black and you may find that some of it sticks to them!'

Bliss's eyes filled with tears and she turned her head away from him, fighting back the tears, not wanting them to spill and show their marks on her face.

What a situation they were in! Two people not long married, and already their antagonism was as palpable as the cold thud of the rain on the roof of their bridal car.

CHAPTER EIGHT

WHEN they boarded the caique the wedding guests were already assembled to greet them, and Bliss realised why the drive had seemed so endless; the driver had been told to take the long way to the harbour so there would be friends on board the *Stella Maris* when they arrived.

Bliss acted her way through the reception; she wore a mask that smiled and concealed the fiery anguish inside her, which was only momentarily cooled by the vintage champagne which flowed freely during those two hours before the guests departed.

Kara Savidge had given Bliss a warm and understanding hug, and had looked directly into her eyes when she said: 'One day, Bliss, come and visit Lucan and myself on our island. There are acres of furniture-wood trees and the beach is a dream. I would very much like you to meet our twin sons, Terence and Shaun ... and if it turns out that you come alone, then rest assured that being with us on Dragon Bay will make things seem better.'

As silence settled down and the caique set sail for Dovima, Bliss stood by the rail and remembered Kara's invitation. If only she were miles away on that other island right now! Miles from this marriage which held only material benefits and withheld the deeper riches of love.

The rain had died away and the sun had returned to bathe the sea in its golden light. The water flickered and danced as the caique skimmed on her way, custom-built so she was longer than was normal for this Greek type of sea-going craft. She was wider, with more accommodation below deck. Her paintwork gleamed and on her side was a glowing star representative of her name, which meant Sea Star. The caique was inlaid with rich mahogany, the king of woods, and there was in the furnishings that air of Victorian comfort and olde-worlde charm which Bliss had noticed at the Club Cassandra.

Her hands clenched the timbered rail and she felt the seething emotions inside her. Not a detail of that evening at the club was missing from her memory. She saw Paris again, standing there against the burgundy curtains, tall and resolute ... allowing her to trap herself in the delusion that he meant her to repay with her body what Justin had embezzled from him.

In the strangest way it was harder to accept that Paris had allowed her to delude herself. She had wanted ... needed to believe that he was as black-hearted as he was black-haired. That he was just a tricky Greek gaming-club owner ... now she stood upon the deck of his caique in Greek waters and the truth was like a thrusting pain that was actually physical.

Everything whirled ... broken pieces of the marriage service spun through her mind, and then suddenly she was falling and couldn't stop herself. Falling through space towards the water, her scream dying away behind her as she hit the sea and fell through a tumult of liquid jade shards.

The shock took away her breath and her mind went black ... she came to with sunlight flickering on her face, and there above her was a grim masculine face, water dripping down on her skin from his wet black hair. Involuntarily her body thrashed there on the deck and she retched sea-water. Hard hands held her as, dizzy and nauseated, she choked out the water which left her feeling drained even as she lay there in her soaking dress.

Paris swore a dark oath as he watched her. 'I had no idea,' he said grimly, 'that your unhappiness was quite so desperate.'

Bliss blinked her eyelashes, and felt an exhaustion that made her hang like a dead weight in his arms when he lifted her and carried her down to the main cabin; she felt herself being lowered and then that light in her mind went dim again and she blacked out. She revived to the sting of cognac on her mouth and to the feel of an arm holding her firmly.

As the cognac warmed her chilled body she realised that she was naked inside a cocoon of blankets. 'D-did you take m-my clothes off?' she asked, rather foolishly.

'You don't imagine I called in one of the crew to remove them, do you?' His eyes above her were menacing; the anger in them was more deadly than any flash of temper. 'You damn little fool, dropping into the sea from a height could have given you cardiac arrest!'

As if in slow motion Bliss mulled over his words, then she felt a jolt of recollection and seemed to feel again the shock and impact of hitting the water. 'I—I must have passed out,' she said faintly. 'I know I felt dizzy——'

'No.' As he shook his head drops of water spattered her face. 'You pitched yourself overboard.'

'No——' Bliss shook her head wildly. 'I wouldn't do such a thing——'

'Wouldn't you?' He fixed his eyes upon her white face, his teeth gritted. 'Fortunately I heard you scream and dived in after you—I enjoyed leaping into the sea on my wedding day in order to drag my foolish bride back on board the caique. What in the name of the gods possessed you?'

She shook her head tiredly. 'Would I scream?' she said wonderingly, but she couldn't be sure what had happened. Her mind had been going round and round—she had been totally lost in her thoughts, there at the rail while he was at the wheel in discussion with a member of the crew.

She felt as if she had been swept into a whirlpool, and tiredly she rubbed her shoulder which ached as if Paris had roughly gripped her in the water.

'You are hurt?' He removed her hand from her shoulder and as he took a look he caught his breath. 'You are bruised there ... I must have done it when I hauled you in.'

'Y-you make me sound like a fish!' She gave a sudden laugh that was half a sob. 'I—I'm sorry, Paris —perhaps I had t-too much champagne and it got mixed up with—with all that incense in the church. It's all been a little too much for me——'

'Too much for you, milady?' He thrust his fingers through her bedraggled hair. 'How do you think I feel? I find it unforgivable that you should go and do such a thing!'

'Paris——' Her gaze was riveted to his face. 'I—I don't remember doing it on purpose——'

'I know what you wanted.' The words emerged grimly from the bar of his teeth. 'You wanted to float away from the moorings of our marriage, but nothing is as easy as that. Even as your mind directed your action your body repudiated it and you screamed for help. What if I had let you go, down into those Aegean depths?'

Bliss felt a pang of terror at the very idea, and though she couldn't tell him how she had come to fall into the sea, she knew that she hadn't leapt in deliberately.

He stood up and turned away from her and she saw a tremor go snaking down his body. 'You're so wet!' she exclaimed. 'You should go and change out of your suit—it's dripping water everywhere——'

'I might catch my death of cold, my dear.' He flung the harsh words over his shoulder. 'Wouldn't that be a better solution for you? You would have my wealth to go with your widow's weeds!'

'Paris—oh, what a thing to say!' She recoiled from his remark. 'As if I wish you dead——'

'Don't you?' He swung to face her and his features were suddenly lit by a lurid flash of lightning through the porthole. The rain had washed out the sun again and brought with it a sea storm. The lightning flared and retreated, and Bliss was huddled in her blankets, her face colourless in the frame of her damp hair.

'What did you do with my wedding dress?' she found herself asking.

'Your wedding dress?' he echoed her, ironically. 'Why should you be interested?'

A flush took the pallor from her face. 'It was a nice dress—it must be spoiled.'

'Quite spoiled,' he agreed, 'just like everything else.'

Bliss watched him in silence as he moved towards the door. 'Try and get some sleep,' he said, 'and don't let the storm worry you. The *Stella Maris* is built to take a buffeting, and I'll awaken you when we reach Dovima.'

'Paris!'

'You wish to say something?' He didn't turn to look at her, a tall man upright with pride in the dark suit that was soggy with sea-water, the white shirt no longer crisp.

'I'm sorry,' was all Bliss found to say.

'Sleep,' he ordered, 'forget!'

He was gone with those words, closing the cabin door firmly behind him, Bliss lay down, uncaring that her hair was still damp. She curled into herself and watched the lightning as it came and went, and listened to the thunder as it rolled over the sea. The caique began to sway to the motion of the storm-lashed water and like a great cradle it finally rocked her off to sleep.

She was awakened by Paris as he had promised; the cabin lamps were alight and the caique was no longer swaying back and forth. Paris had changed into a high-necked black sweater and dark trousers, and he held a steaming mug of coffee. 'Come, sit up and drink this, then get dressed. The island is hoving in sight and we should arrive in about fifteen minutes.'

Bliss pushed herself into a sitting position and accepted the coffee from him. Her throat felt parched, which was probably the result of swallowing sea-water, and gratefully she drank the hot sweet coffee.

'Come on deck when you are ready,' said Paris, then he was gone again, making Bliss realise that he was behaving like a stranger. Anyway, the coffee enlivened her and when she slid from the bunk she found that her legs were fairly stable. Her suitcases had been brought on board the caique, from the hotel in Athens, while she had been in church with Paris, so she had no problem in finding underwear, a blouse and a suit to replace her ruined wedding dress. She went into the bathroom to freshen up and to do something about her hair, but the dress and the dainty underthings which had matched it in fabric and colour were nowhere to be seen.

As she combed her hair in front of the mirror she supposed that Paris had flung them overboard in his raging anger, and as she gazed into her reflected eyes she had again the bewildered feeling that she hadn't dropped into the sea on purpose.

She half-turned to the mirror so she could get a glimpse of her right shoulder, which still ached ... the reflected bruise was fairly large and a

deep purple colour. She was aware that she
always bruised dramatically, and could only
suppose once again that Paris had unintentionally
hurt her when he had rescued her from the water.

As she stood there a tremor shook her body. It
was alarming to discover that she was capable of
an action which her mind refused to remember.
Madame Lilian had once explained to her that
human beings were sometimes at the mercy of
impulses they didn't fully understand; driven to
actions unrelated to their normal behaviour
because of some traumatic event in their lives
that they couldn't cope with.

Bliss arranged her hair at the nape of her neck,
then applied a little make-up that made her look
less wan, and five minutes later she was mounting
the staircase to the deck of the *Stella Maris*. She
was miles removed from those rooms in
Westminster where Madame Lilian read the
Tarot cards and tried to pierce the veils which
shrouded each person's destiny.

There at the deckside in the shape of a tall,
dark figure stood Bliss's destiny, and she went
across to his side as the caique sailed towards the
cliffs of Dovima. Following the storm the sun
was setting in a dramatic web of deep flame and
gold veined by purple, like the bruising of Bliss's
shoulder. Those cliffs were as if sculpted out of
petrified flame, and the vivid beauty of the scene
took her breath away.

The prow of the caique broke through the
dusky-gold water, and Paris gave her an
impersonal glance. 'These islands,' he told her,
'were once the trade marts of the Venetians, and

also their naval bases. In daylight Dovima basks in the sea like a great golden lion; a lonely island which appealed to me.'

He had used the word lonely once before, and Bliss realised how strongly it applied to him despite his financial successes which enabled him to mingle with people who enjoyed the social life. This island in the Aegean was more his world than the club in Curzon Street, or the house on the Yorkshire moors where Bliss longed to be.

The caique rounded the headland of the island's bay, where she was anchored, a boat being lowered so she and her husband could be rowed ashore beneath the thrusting power of the cliffs that guarded the island.

A cliffside elevator carried them up to the headland, where a Range Rover waited to take them to the villa. A manservant with black curly hair sat at the wheel, and every now and again as they drove over rather bumpy ground he cast a curious look at Bliss. So this, his look seemed to say, was the English bride of his Greek master ... this pale-faced girl in a mink coat, huddled into the rich fur as if she were cold.

Where was her smile, and why did she sit apart from her bridegroom when she should have been close to his side?

Bliss knew the questions that were going through that Greek head. She had seen one of the sailors on the caique looking at her in a similar way, almost glowering as he had served champagne to the wedding guests, as if these people strongly disapproved of having her as their *kyria*.

She understood their feelings; she was as

loyally English as they were Greek ... of course
they would have preferred their master to marry
a girl of their own kind, dark-haired and brown-
limbed, who was akin to all this vivid wildness of
sea and scenery.

Even as she was thinking this Bliss was
resenting their judgment of her. They should see
her on horseback riding the moors, with her hair
blowing in the wind and her eyes alight with
pleasure in the place and the gallop. In her own
surroundings she was as alive and vital as any
Greek girl. She had loved those long, idyllic
summers, with the gorse growing high on the
slopes of the moorlands. She'd be out of the
house at the break of dawn, not wanting to waste
a moment of each day, young and carefree and
unaware of the gambling fever in her father that
was laying waste her heritage and Justin's.

She gave a sudden start when she felt Paris
grip her hand. 'In a while you will see the old
Venetian walls that surround the villa; they were
still intact and it would have been criminal to
knock down such walls. *Pedhi mou*, how cold
your hand is! I hope you haven't caught a chill;
what a damper that would put on our honeymoon!'

Bliss felt him looking at her, and the fact that
his concern was related to his own expectation of
pleasure made her grit her teeth; she could hardly
bear to be what she was to him, an object of
desire that he anticipated owning, just as he
owned this island and the villa he had built upon
it.

Suddenly the Range Rover turned in between

tall stone posts from which high cobbled walls stretched around the villa. 'We arrive!' Paris exclaimed. 'We are home!'

It was he who arrived home; Bliss felt miles from everything that was familiar to her. He leapt eagerly from the vehicle as soon as it stopped and there was a sound of barking as a shaggy old lion of a dog hurled itself at Paris, great paws planted on him, huge tail wagging back and forth.

'Ajax, my old friend, I have missed you as well!' Paris turned to Bliss with a flash of white teeth. 'He's a gentle old giant, so don't be afraid of him.'

'I never have been afraid of anything on four legs,' she rejoined, and quite without fear she patted the great dog and allowed him to sniff at her fur coat, which he abruptly nuzzled, almost knocking her off her feet.

'Mind your manners or I'll turn you into a rug!' Paris thrust an arm about Bliss and gestured at the villa. 'Not Cathlamet, perhaps, but pleasing enough, wouldn't you say?'

Her smile was reticent; wall lamps threw mysterious shadows on to the walls and windows of the large Greek house, and the night air smelled of pine-trees. Bliss took a deep, steadying breath and felt better for it.

'My *kastello*,' Paris murmured. 'My sea-castle built upon the ruins of an old Venetian fort, but inside it has modern amenities and comfortable beds.'

It seemed to Bliss that he dwelt upon these two words, and though she refrained from looking at him, she suspected that he wore the sardonic

smile that didn't quite reach into his eyes. They
entered the villa through a cavernous front door,
set deep because the walls were thick, a Greek
precaution against earthquake. Gaily-coloured
rugs lay across a slate-stone floor at the centre of
which was a huge keystone which Bliss was
informed was a symbol of welcome.

The hall was so long that the end of it was lost
in shadows, but at the centre there was a minaret
stove frilled by wrought-iron and panelled with
mosaic tiles. 'I find those Turkish stoves
fascinating and the warmth is needed in the
wintertime,' said Paris, stroking a hand across the
tiling.

Bliss glanced about her wide-eyed, and beneath
windows and lamps of jewel-coloured glass she
saw a great fur flung across a couch which looked
big enough to seat half a dozen people. It looked,
in fact, like the couch of a barbarian . . . her heart
thumped as she realised anew that there was a
strain of the East in the man who had built this
house and furnished it to his heart's content. The
slatiness in his nature was shot through by layers
of a richer, more sensual quality.

Oh, how very different from Cathlamet, with
its sombre, oaken atmosphere within the
Yorkstone walls. Bliss wanted to find fault with
this house on the island of Dovima, but her
senses betrayed her and she found herself
fascinated by the overall effect of silver-framed
ikons displayed upon a side-table which matched
other pieces of solid, hand-carved furniture.

Flickers of silver and jewelled lamplight, and
furniture reflecting a dark-purplish sheen against

sheer white walls into which the windows were set so deep that the sills were invitingly heaped with cushions in a pavilion of darkly rich drapes.

Followed by servants with the baggage they went upstairs her hand trailing the frescoed iron. At the head of the staircase Bliss glanced down into the hall, taking in again the strangeness of it all.

An almost Byzantine beauty, as if Paris needed to compensate for his boyhood which had been so Spartan. 'Aren't you impressed?' he asked, with a touch of irony.

'Well, you called this place your castle,' she rejoined. 'Yours to make your very own, a reflection of your personality, and men of the East have always guarded their treasures within plain walls, haven't they?'

'So now you see it?' He drew her gaze to his face and she was potently aware of his darkness clothed darkly, intensifying all the differences that lay between them . . . background, culture and sex. A wave of weakness swept over her, and it must have shown in her face, for suddenly he swept her up in his arms and carried her the rest of the way to the huge bedroom beyond doors fit for a chapel.

CHAPTER NINE

So here she was at the villa where her honeymoon was to take place; that romantic time of discovery which was sometimes a joy, sometimes a disappointment even for newlyweds who cared deeply for each other.

Bliss cooled her skin from an atomiser of toilet water, and through the mirror of the vanity-table she could see the bed in its frame of filmy net draping the Oriental wood embellished with mother-of-pearl. A Turkish bed, she had been informed, and there had lain in Paris's eyes that faintly mocking smile when she had not been able to control herself from looking away from the bed.

'Straight out of a *seraglio*, I imagine,' she had commented.

She blotted her lips so they wouldn't look too glaring against her paleness and went over to take her dress from its hanger; a silver-green dress that shimmered here and there with charming bead embroidery. She stepped into it and drew it up over her body, closing the concealed zip in the side. Little silver clips shaped like leaves held her hair in a thick soft knot, and after a moment of hesitation she clipped on the pearls which she had worn at her wedding . . . pearls for tears, she thought, fingering them.

The strand of pearls were all that had remained

on her body after Paris had stripped her of her wet clothes on the *Stella Maris*, and she wore them tonight almost as a gesture of fatalism.

Aspasia the maid came into the bedroom, carrying the cup of tea Bliss had asked for. She had packed a box of English tea in her suitcase, unable to face the prospect of an entire fortnight without her favourite brew. Coffee was all right, but it always left her feeling thirsty; she much preferred a good cup of tea and accepted the steaming cup with a grateful murmur of thanks.

Already she had discovered that Aspasia had a little broken English, so they were able to converse after a fashion. The young woman had told her that her regular duties were involved with the mother of the *kyrios*, but she was to wait upon Bliss during the next two weeks.

She was striking to look at, with her dark hair braided across the crown of her head and wearing a full-sleeved dress and a frilled white apron.

There in that marble grotto of a bathroom she had been in and out while Bliss bathed, intent, it seemed, on catching full sight of the pale-skinned English girl when she climbed out from among the peach-scented bubbles.

Bliss had fooled her. She had asked for the tea, knowing very well that in a Greek household it wouldn't be easy for the cook to find a suitable pot in which to brew the tea. She smiled to herself as she sipped from her cup; as a working girl she was accustomed to bathing and dressing quickly in order to catch her bus each morning.

She felt Aspasia looking her over in the silver-green dress, which like the rest of her trousseau was made to perfection in a style and a colour that suited Bliss's colouring.

She enjoyed the freedom of the bathroom because Paris had a sauna of his own and also a squash court, he told her, where she was welcome to join him in the mornings. He had slapped his flat stomach when he spoke, an indication that he meant it to stay that way.

'You have beautiful clothes, *kyria*.' Aspasia went over to the big, alcoved cupboard where they had been installed and the fabrics rustled as she moved the dresses and other outfits. She turned again to face Bliss and her dark eyes had narrowed in a rather calculating way.

'It was not known that the *kyrios* was to be married—it took his mother greatly by surprise,' Aspasia spoke each English word in a deliberate way that seemed to add a significance Bliss didn't fail to notice.

'I—I hope Madame Apollonaris wasn't too— upset?' she asked.

Aspasia shrugged her shoulders and raised a hand to touch the glossy braided hair. 'The *kyrios* is everything to her—she wept that evening when the news was brought across on the caique, which goes back and forth to collect provisions and mail from the post office.'

'I see.' Bliss swirled the tea-leaves at the bottom of her cup and wished that like Madame Lilian she could read them and find some message of hope regarding this marriage which Paris had forced upon his mother as well as herself.

'I—I'm sorry the news upset her. I realise that

it must have been unexpected, but she was very gracious to me at the church. I thought her a very nice woman.'

'She is a very Greek woman,' Aspasia said deliberately.

'Meaning that she would have preferred her son to marry a Greek girl,' said Bliss, hoping that her features were more composed than her inner feelings, which had been in a tumult all day long. 'I do understand how Madame Apollonaris feels; I know the news was sprung on her.'

Bliss knew it now, and wished fervently that she hadn't been so quick to misjudge Paris during that interview at the Club Cassandra, when the beat of the rain had seemed to play on her nerves, so strung up ever since Justin had informed her of what he had been doing to the club's books; getting deeper in debt as he tried to win back his losses until the embezzled sum had grown into figures that Justin could no longer juggle.

Justin had been so certain that Paris would have him arrested . . . he had pleaded with Bliss to do something, anything that would stay Paris's hand.

Bliss gazed at her own right hand where the golden ring was still so gleaming and new, and wide-banded as if determined to display itself.

'It is known,' Aspasia's voice broke in on Bliss's thoughts, 'that in England people marry without the long engagement.'

'Yes——' Bliss looked across at the maid, and it suddenly struck her what was being implied . . . Paris was a rich Greek, the kind of man a lot of women would aim to marry in order to live well and have lots of beautiful clothes, not to mention jewellery.

The assumption brought a flash of temper into Bliss's eyes so they sparkled diamond-grey, and angry words were trembling on her lips when the tall doors of the bedroom were thrust open to admit Paris, tall and imposing in a dinner-suit, his shirtfront agleam against his swarthy skin.

'I come to fetch you to dinner—ah, I see you are dressed and ready!'

His eyes scanned Bliss from her silvery hair down to the silver tips of her shoes beneath the hem of the silvery-green dress.

'Delightful!' He held out a hand to her. 'You look like the sea-goddess Aphrodite.'

Bliss's flash of anger had enlivened her and she was aware of it as she crossed the room to join Paris. The beadwork of her dress shimmered and she could feel a pulsing in her body and legs as she went downstairs with him.

No doubt Aspasia was attached to Madame Apollonaris and had grown used to being familiar with her, but Bliss told herself that she wasn't being placed in the position of defending her right to be in this house. She didn't want to make an enemy of Aspasia, but that young woman was going to have to be shown that she wasn't welcome as a personal attendant.

It was true that Bliss had grown up in a household where there were servants, but that was in the past, and only Nanny Davis had been allowed to be familiar with her remarks.

'Paris,' she said, 'I don't need a maid. Why

don't you give Aspasia a holiday so she can go to Athens?'

'But that would offend my mother.' He gave her a rather quizzical look and paused with her upon that great keystone at the centre of the hall, above which a great lamp showered them with its light. 'Aspasia was left here to wait upon you, and from your appearance she has done a good job.'

'I dressed myself,' Bliss said tartly. 'I don't need a maid, and besides that——'

A frown drew his brows together as she broke off, biting on her lower lip. 'Has Aspasia said something out of turn?' Paris demanded.

'I don't like telling tales,' Bliss tilted her chin and a flash of temper shimmered in her eyes again. 'Your people think I've married you for your money, if you must know!'

'Is that all?' He looked ironic. 'What a smack in the eye for me, when I had hoped that people would think you had married me for my charming ways!'

'Paris, it's all very well for you to make a joke of it, but I don't like being labelled a gold-digger!'

'Whatever label you are wearing, *pedhaki mou*, you look as if you are worth every pound of it.' He took her hand in his, with just enough firmness to let her know that she had better leave it there. 'Come, when you have eaten dinner you will feel more relaxed and less inclined to care what people say about either of us.'

'Aspasia told me that your mother was extremely upset when she received the news that you were going to marry me—an English girl.'

'No doubt.' He drew her towards the dining-room. 'But she was friendly towards you in church, was she not? My mother is Greek, therefore she is fatalistic and accepts what has to be.'

'What is, Paris, is what you've made it,' Bliss rejoined. 'I'm here at your command and you know it very well.'

'Perhaps so.' He withdrew a tall-backed chair from the table laid for two and invited her to be seated. As Bliss lowered herself into the chair, Paris lowered his head and brushed her profile with his lips.

'You have haunting cheekbones, do you know it?' His warm breath fanned her skin and she strove to remain calm and fixed her gaze upon the lovely spray of flowers at the centre of the table.

'Don't you like me to pay you compliments?' He sat down in the chair facing hers, and the centrepiece of flowers was so arranged that he could look directly across at her.

'I daresay you feel you have to make them,' she replied, her voice low and cool. 'I expect you've had quite a bit of practice in the art of lowering a girl's defences.'

'Ah, is that what I'm doing, Bliss? I thought I was behaving like a man on his honeymoon.'

Her skin warmed, casting a radiance over her cheekbones that wasn't reflected inside her. She couldn't help but look at Paris, and there was no doubt that he possessed that indefinable quality known as presence. He had certainly mastered the art of sophistication, for it was hard to detect in him that scruffy little boy that other children had jeered at, and even thrown stones at. Bliss tried not to think of that thin, dark-haired boy with the lonely eyes . . . tonight it was a man who sat looking at her, and his eyes were possessive.

'Tomorrow,' he said, 'I'll show you over Dovima. The Venetians left their traces all over these islands; they were crusaders and captains of fortune; traders and invaders. You might say that the Lion of Saint Mark left its mark for nearly three hundred years upon the islands in Greek waters . . . in all of us there are traces of forgotten races, when you come to think about it.'

All through dinner Paris did most of the talking and Bliss listened to him with interest; he was extremely well read, she realised, and had fed his astute mind with all sorts of knowledge. He knew the history of York and had wandered all over the beautiful Minster and had attended Evensong there, something Bliss had often done.

The wine they drank with their meal was the colour of a dark red rose, and its effect upon Bliss was to make her feel more relaxed, and she had to admit to herself that Paris captured her imagination even if he eluded her understanding.

When they had finished their dessert of coffee ice-cream garnished with roasted walnuts, they went to take coffee in a white and gold *saloni* that Bliss couldn't help but admire. Across the floor lay a carpet of a thousand flowers and overhead were crystal chandeliers like so many glass flowers with delicate branches of glass leaves. The furniture was of pale golden wood, with deep tawny velvet armchairs, and rich ivory curtains framed windows that were letting in a scent so familiar to her.

She took a deep breath and felt herself wafted back to Cathlamet, where a great patch of crimson nicotiana grew beneath the windows of the sitting-room, wafting in their scent when the evenings were mild and the windows open.

'It can't be,' she murmured. 'Does nicotiana grow in Greece?'

'It does now,' Paris replied. 'I had a patch of the plant uprooted from the garden at Cathlamet and replanted here in Greek soil, shaded by those trees beyond the windows so the sun wouldn't burn the roots. It seems to have worked, eh?'

Bliss gave him a startled look. 'What a—a surprising thing to do!'

'Surprising?' He arched an eyebrow. 'Do you think me so hard and unimaginative?'

'You do give that impression.' She seated herself so she was half-turned away from him, that nostalgic breath of England in her nostrils, her profile framed cameo-like against the tawny wing of her chair.

'Even tonight do I give it?' he asked, long legs straddling the carpet in which myriad flowers were woven, colours and shapes blending in the thick wool, the work of a subtle Eastern weaver.

Bliss refused to look at him even though she could feel his eyes compelling her attention. 'It's part of you . . . you wouldn't be Paris Apollonaris if you allowed your heart to overrule your head.'

'So at least you admit that I have a heart.'

'Hasn't everyone?' She forced a cool and dispassionate note into her voice, a match for the ice-maiden look which had always kept her brother's friends at bay; rowdy young men who came to Cathlamet and left her quite unmoved. She had much preferred to leap into the saddle of her favourite horse and ride the moors alone. No, those young men couldn't disturb her . . . unlike the tall, dark Greek who had taken her for his own in that gilded church where the incense smoked and the candle flames shimmered in the beaten silver ikons.

The exotic rituals of her marriage still clung to her senses, not even dispelled by the scent of the tobacco flowers which had taken root in the garden of this Greek house on an island, where she felt isolated with him despite the few people he had working on the premises. To them her British fairness was strange and alien . . . she was the icy girl who must melt in the brown, warm-skinned arms of their *kyrios*.

Suddenly Bliss became aware that Paris had crossed the room and was standing behind her chair; he had that unaware, silent suppleness of animals, probably a part of him from childhood when out on the hills he would run with the goats and curl up with them in order to share their warmth beneath the stars.

She tensed when he cradled her neck with his hands, his fingers touching her pearls. 'I'm pleased you wore these tonight.' He leaned down so his breath stirred her hair. 'They remind me of how you looked in the church this morning—do you feel married, *moiya*?'

The pulse in her neck beat fast beneath his touch . . . the possessive touch of a husband. 'Don't do that!' Quite unable to control her panic, Bliss jumped to her feet and backed away from him, just as if he was an animal that threatened her. The pupils of her eyes were so dilated that they looked as if filled with his threatening shadow.

'Are you asking me not to come near you?' He spoke with a deceptive quietness, and he stood there with a deceptive stillness, his gaze fixed upon her face that was pale as the pearls around her neck. 'Come, Bliss, isn't that asking a little too much of a bridegroom?'

'Y-you know how I feel about you——' She didn't want to plead or grovel, so she did the next best thing and fled through the windows that stood open to the moonshot night and the heady scent of nicotine flowers. She rushed along the stone terrace clutching the long skirt of her dress as she made for a flight of steps leading down into the garden. She had no real hope of escaping him, but at least she could show him that she didn't want to be with him. If he had any pride, then surely he wouldn't force himself upon her!

A stranger to the garden, she didn't know where she was going, and suddenly she found herself on a kind of patio where the pale shadows of broken statuary stood among the trees. It was as if she was in a garden of ghosts and at any other time she might have found herself fascinated.

Her momentary pause in front of a male statue that was quite faceless had given Paris time to catch up with her, and she gave a little choked cry when his hands closed upon her shoulders and he spun her to face him. The moonlight sheened her hair but drained her skin, and she hung there in his hands as if expecting him to exert his marital rights here among the cold stone figures.

His fingers gripped her, as if he were reading her fears in her eyes. 'Do you quite hate me?' he asked. 'I am a Greek and I don't intend to spend my wedding night in a lonely bed. When a man takes a wife his nights alone are ended, and here in the light of the moon your eyes are a book I read and your lips are a well from which I want to drink. Come, *pedhaki mou*, slip into my arms and be one with me—forget everything else and just be my woman.'

Forget ... how could she ever forget that he had bought her, that he owned her, his possession like this island and Cathlamet brooding among its stone walls on the wild and lovely moors?

A sigh caught in her throat, turning to a little cry as Paris lifted her into his arms and strode with her through the garden and up the steps, not a man of stone like those figures, but a warm, sensual and determined human being.

The urge to fight him was strong in her, but he was far stronger and she decided that the best defence was to remain quite passive. A man of his passions would want a responsive partner in his arms, not a woman who listlessly accepted him.

They arrived in the bedroom and there he set her upon her feet; a swift glance had shown Bliss that the sheets were turned back in the soft glimmer of bedside lamps and her nightdress and robe of broderie arabe were laid out.

Bliss could feel her pounding heart, realising that for the first time since she reached womanhood she wasn't going to have privacy in her bedroom any more. Paris had the right to come and go as the mood took him. He could watch her undress if that was his wish. He could enter the bathroom while she bathed ... he was the most intimate of people ... he was Paris, her husband.

They stood facing each other in silence, utterly alone together after the excitements of their wedding day. Bliss was unaware that her eyes were pleading with him, that in the tremor of her lips there were unspoken words appealing for the clemency he wouldn't grant. A Greek from the crown of his dark head to the soles of his feet, to whom a wife was flesh of his flesh.

'I know you are feeling shy of me,' he broke the silence in a low-toned voice, then gestured towards the far door that connected with another room. 'I shall leave you for a while so you can prepare yourself for bed. Don't go to sleep, my Bliss, for I shall awaken you.'

She watched motionless as he walked to that arched door, set deep like all the doors in this house, and drew it open to reveal a white-walled, almost monastic room, with a low couch covered by a black and white blanket, and with shaggy rugs upon a wooden floor. Then the door closed behind him and Bliss was alone, with his words left stranded in the air she quickly breathed.

She looked around her as if seeking a way to escape him, but this was a house on an island and leagues of star-spattered ocean lay between her and the mainland.

There was nothing else to do but accept that she was a bride and this was her wedding night.

She felt a pulsing of alarm through her body, a girl who had sheltered her feelings; who had never indulged in those fumblings and follies that brought a measure of awareness to many other girls facing a husband for the first time.

To the tempestuous beat of her heart she prepared for bed. The broderie arabe night robe had endless tiny buttons all the way down the front, and with fumbling fingers Bliss deliberately buttoned each one until she felt encased in the embroidered lace. Then she went to the mirror and studied herself ... a slim stranger in lots of lace, the vanity lamps shining in her hair and making blue-gold pools of her eyes.

So be it, she thought, holding her body very still and straight as Paris returned to her room, a tall figure in matt black, the robe loosely tied so it was open against his strong chest where the hair was crisply black against his skin.

As he came towards her, his eyes focused upon her face, there was an indisputable, animal-like grace about him. Bliss knew that he felt none of her fear or uncertainty, none of her awareness of how untaught she was in the ways of sensuality.

As she stood there in the radiance of the lamps she had an almost breathless purity, her skin and hair combining with the lace to make her so, the look in her eyes that of a novice about to brave the inner mysteries of life.

'How lovely you are!'

For a startled moment she wondered if there had been a note of tenderness in his voice ... a wonderment dispelled when he began with deliberate and steady hands to unbutton her robe, starting at her throat, his gaze holding hers as his fingers moved slowly downwards until he reached the level of her pounding heart.

'The garment becomes you,' he murmured, 'but I want to admire your white skin. I want to touch you, Bliss. I want your silken softness in my arms, where I shall melt you, my girl, even if you hate me in the morning. Even if you regard me as predator rather than lover.'

When he reached the buttons at the level of her hips he swung her on to the bed, holding her with a thrust of his leg as he rapidly unbuttoned the robe to the hem.

She lay there in the delicate lace of the nightdress, and suddenly he leaned over her and buried his lips in the silky warmth below her collarbone.

'Are you going to make me take you?' he breathed. 'Is that the way you want our wedding night?'

She gazed up at him, into the eyes that were so penetrating in the sun-darkened face. She felt his hands sliding over the silky softness of her body, there beneath the sheath of lace that was her only concealment.

With a kind of desperation she strove not to feel anything; she turned aside her face, teeth pressing down into her lip as she heard the slither of his robe as he removed it. Then she felt his warm skin against hers, felt his lips caressing the sensitive sides of her breasts. Her throat pulsed, caging the moan of pleasure that wanted to escape.

Bliss hadn't known that her own body could

betray her in this way, wanting the hands and the warm and lingering mouth that touched her, knowing her body as she had never known it. His hand fondled lightly, maddeningly, the smooth curve of her stomach, the very tip of a finger stroking the soft scrolling of her navel.

She wanted to hate what he was doing to her, wanted to despise herself for the sweet, heavy need to abandon herself to the body and will of Paris.

His eyes smouldered down into hers, for he hadn't turned off the lamps and she could see the passion and the pleasure in his face as he caressed her until her every nerve was as if tipped with a flame. She had believed ... hoped that in being passive in his arms she would be apart from his possession of her, but with infinite awareness of her sensitivity he coaxed her across the border between restraint and abandon.

He held her captive ... held her with eyes and hands for a long and torturous moment, and then he brought his warm mouth down upon hers and her involuntary cry was silenced in the deep centre of his kiss. She had an incredible moment of awareness. 'I shall never belong to myself again ... I am possessed by Paris!'

He was invasive ... he was hurting her, and she tried to push him away from her. 'Hush, don't do that,' he breathed, and holding her in the cradle of his hands he brought about the abandonment he had sought from her from the beginning of the lovemaking.

She lay in the enclosure of his arms, feeling the incredible male force of him. Words in Greek and

English spilled into her ears, and her body arched to his and her fingers plunged deep into his black hair and there was not a thing in the world, nobody beyond this tumultuous union of their two selves.

Paris didn't fall asleep until daylight came soft and cool against the windows, a strong arm and a long leg flung across the slim body in his arms.

Bliss lay there languorously, listening to Paris as he breathed, feeling the small movements he made in his sleep. Tentatively she touched his warm skin, curious about the tawny, tigerish body which had subdued and finally brought her to culminations of delight and excitement. A delight far more acute than the initial pain of his possession of her, her supple young body so awakened by him that she was left with a glow at the centre of herself, though in every sort of way she had been virginal.

Even her mind had been uncluttered by images of men with women, and only fleetingly had she wondered how people could bring themselves to be so abandoned to each other. It had seemed to her a rather undignified way to express affection and she had concluded that wives calmly submitted to the desires of their menfolk and didn't share in the sensuality which took no heed of dignity and doubt and had a wild kind of grandeur ... like the sea in tumult ... like a storm at its height ... primative and untameable.

Bliss knew that Paris had enjoyed her with the thoroughness of his Greek nature, and from a girl he had made her into a woman. Carefully she drew her fingers down the strong wall of his chest, feeling his heartbeat beneath the vibrant dark hair. A shiver of emotion ran through her body, fluttering the nerves in the pit of her stomach. He was so ineffably his own master, and all through the night he had been hers. In sleep he looked remote though their skins were warmly touching, the closed-down eyelids concealed those fires which had smoked and burned in his eyes . . . he had taught her that the passions of the body weren't shameful, and finally, without shame, or inhibition, or the memory of why they had married, she had clung to the naked power of his shoulders and surrendered herself to him.

A slightly wondering smile touched her lips as she fell asleep, with his whipcord arm binding her to him. She was now the property of Paris Apollonaris, and what was his he took and held with all the tenacity of a man who had used wits and brawn to build a life on the rocks of poverty.

Silvery-haired Bliss, with her soft curve of a mouth and her slim white body, belonged to the one man in the world whom she had tried to evade, and he held her to him as if sleep was dangerous . . . as if while he slept she might escape from his possession.

CHAPTER TEN

BLISS awoke a long time later to find Aspasia at her bedside. She was holding a laden tray of food and gazing down intently, so their eyes met the moment Bliss stirred into wakefulness.

Pushing the tousled hair from her brow, Bliss sat up and found her cheeks flooding with warmth under the Greek woman's gaze. She knew there was an old tradition relating to Greek bridals and fervently hoped that it wasn't going to be carried out ... though there was every chance that Paris's mother had secretly asked Aspasia to ensure that her son's bride had been virginal.

'The *kyria* has slept very well,' Aspasia murmured, and it was a statement rather than a query.

'Yes——' Bliss glanced a the bedside clock and couldn't suppress a gasp when she saw the time. It was three o'clock in the afternoon and the hot Greek sun was held at bay by the louvred shutters and a large fan spun its blades in the centre of the ceiling, cooling the air. 'Oh, my gracious, is that really the time!'

'Every moment of it.' Aspasia didn't smile as she spoke. 'I have brought luncheon to the *kyria* as breakfast is long over. Will you eat in bed, madame?'

'No, I must go and shower.' Bliss flung aside

the covers, forgetful that her lace nightdress had
been removed hours ago, and a blush swept her
nude white body as she felt the inquisitive flick of
the maid's dark eyes.

She hastened past Aspasia and went into the
bathroom, calling over her shoulder that she
would take lunch on the balcony.

Beneath the shower each moment of the night
recurred, and with an almost unaware sensu-
ousness she stroked the scented foam over
herself, remembering how Paris had kissed each
curve, each secret dip and swell with lingering
lips.

Nerves rippled low down in her stomach and
her eyelids felt weighted by her sensual thoughts.
There was no denying the pleasure she had felt in
those strong, possessive arms. Paris was every
inch a man, and he had taken her on a journey of
the body which had been incredibly exciting.

And it would happen again, she thought, as she
towelled her body. Again, and yet again, she
would lie in his arms and he would make
passionate love to her. And she would want his
passion . . . would revel in his lips speaking fierce
little words in Greek, and gazing into her wide-
pupilled eyes in the wall mirror Bliss wondered
if he had forced his way into her heart.

It was something she couldn't know . . .
something she hardly dared to think about until
in a while she saw him again. Love was such a
mystery, such a strange and awesome emotion,
and she had read in books that infatuation could
be mistaken for love. That the body could rule
the mind.

In the Greek church yesterday she had felt a
stranger at the altar, surrounded by the wedding
guests. On the *Stella Maris* she had felt so
despairing that it had affected her physically and
she had fallen from the caique into the sea.

Slowly she turned the unflawed front of her
body and saw again that bruise on her shoulder
which Paris believed he had inflicted in the water
when he had dived in to save her.

It seemed the only possibility, and yet Bliss
had never thought of Paris as a monster, only as a
force which threatened her freedom and
independence. She wouldn't go so far as to drown
herself in order to escape him ... that kind of
folly wasn't bred into her bones, and yet that
struggle in the Aegean had occurred. She had
found herself in the sea, gasping for breath and
frightened out of her wits.

'Forget!' he had said, and very conclusively
last night he had closed her mind to unhappy
events.

Bliss realised, with a jolt of pure amazement,
that he had simply made her ... happy. And still
that glow was in her body, so that her skin
glowed and her hair shone, while deep in her eyes
there was a spark of gaiety.

She felt as if yesterday had never been. As if
she hadn't been born until last night, and tying
the sash of her robe she returned to the bedroom
where the louvred shutters had been opened to
frame the balcony where a table had been shaded
by a large fringed sunshade and the food laid in
readiness for her.

She went to the balcony edge, where the grille

of iron was hot to the touch. She had never in her life seen such a bountiful sun, making the sea glisten with the deep blue brilliance of sapphires. This was Dovima, cut off from contact with that other life she had known, unaware that it lacked something vital, expectant, thrilling.

Today she was aware of everything ... alive as she had never been before, and she revelled in the feeling, finding every sip of coffee delicious, every bite of food equally so.

It was when she came to the selection of fruit, trying to decide between deep-purple grapes, softly flushed apricots and ripe-fleshed nectarines, that she noticed a thin line dividing one of the big rosy nectarines in two. When she picked it up the halves fell apart and there at the centre, instead of the large stone, lay a foil-wrapped object which she proceeded to unwrap.

Bliss caught her breath, holding the heart-shaped ruby by its slim golden chain, watching how the sun made it glow blood-red.

'I hope you like it?' a voice murmured.

She turned quickly and there was Paris standing in the doorway of the balcony, his skin the colour of teakwood against the white cotton slacks and T-shirt.

'It's gorgeous——' Her breath seemed to be fluttering in her throat as he approached her ... he looked the man he had always been, and she looked exactly the same girl, but after last night everything was changed and the awareness was there in his lazily smiling eyes.

'You slept like a baby, eh?' He leaned over her and involuntarily she raised her lips to meet his, and as he kissed her Paris drew her to her feet and pressed her close against him.

'You are feeling good?' he murmured, a hand stroking her silvery hair, his eyes fondling her face.

She knew what he meant and still she could blush. The smile deepened in his eyes as he drew his fingers down her face, as if enjoying that flow of warmth with his fingertips. 'So you like your pendant?'

She nodded. 'As always you're an unexpected man, Paris.'

'Call it my heart's blood,' he murmured, and taking the pendant from her fingers he hung it about her neck so the ruby lay warmly red against her white skin.

'I always thought you lovely,' he said, his voice sounding extra deep, 'but I look at you now, *moiya*, and there is a glow that warms me and beckons me. Our wedding night, I think, was agreeable to both of us, eh?'

Bliss fondled the ruby heart and met his eyes with a certain shyness, aware with total certainty in that moment that no other man would ever know her as Paris did. She had once asked Madame Lilian if men and women knew each other in lives they had lived before, for right now, in the strangest way, Bliss felt as if she and Paris had stood like this in the sunlight of long, long ago. She felt so aware of him, as if the cells of his skin were hers . . . as if his heartbeats matched her own.

'Yesterday you had fears and regrets,' he said. 'Are they gone—quite gone?'

'Almost,' she said truthfully. 'I shall always regret that Justin stole from you, I can't help myself.'

'You are young, proud and romantic,' he spread his hands speakingly, 'it's understandable. Now the fears, speak of those!'

'I—I shall always be afraid——'

'Afraid, Bliss?'

'That you'll think,' her fingers clenched the ruby, 'that whenever we make love, I'm repaying you——'

An oath escaped him and with alarming strength he reached for her and swung her up into his arms, striding with her into the bedroom. Directly he touched her, lifted her, took her to the bed where they had eclipsed each other's less than happy memories, the need was there again to find pleasure and forget pain.

The emotional fires smouldered between them as their lips clung and he slowly lowered her to the bed, which had been stripped and remade with cool, lemon-scented sheets.

'Ah, the sweet fire of these eyes.' Paris enclosed her face with his hands and searched her eyes for a long, breathless moment. Her eyes were dreamy, her lips apart in readiness for his kisses even as she murmured:

'We mustn't—not in the middle of the day!'

'This is the time of siesta, my conventional one.' He laughed softly. 'What fool would waste such God-given time, least of all two people like ourselves?'

'Why do you say that, Paris?' She lay there submissively while he drew open the sash of her robe and slid the silk covering from her body, slowly, as if building his anticipation to a peak.

'You and I, *moiya*, have waited a long time to be together.'

'Oh——' Contrition filled her eyes as she watched him peel the T-shirt from his brown torso, as she waited for him to unfasten the thin leather belt that held his slacks. 'You won't forgive me very easily for the first refusal, will you, Paris?'

He shook his head, a figure hewn of tough and durable flesh, and of resolution to match it. 'You wasted precious time for us, child, waiting until that shiftless brother of yours brought you running to me.' He leaned over her and stroked a hand from her throat to her thigh. 'I won't forgive you for the waste of all those siestas we could have spent together as we are about to spend this one.'

'Suppose the maid returns?' Although with words she was denying her own excitement, her body was reacting to his persuasive touch. His power was taking her over and she had no will to resist him. And as if she were a precious object for which he had paid a huge sum he enjoyed her with his eyes even as his hands explored the texture of her skin. Enjoyed the soft curves of her mouth, the pale glimmer of her teeth, the fine clustering lashes that lent sensual mystery to her eyes. Enjoyed the way her hair caught the light, the way the silky scoops beneath her collarbones caught and held shadow.

As she lay there beneath the arch of his chest and shoulders her face had a haunting kind of appeal, as if always with Paris it would be as if they made love for the first time.

'You have such a kissable mouth,' and sensuously he moved his lips against the silky smoothness of hers. 'You have the body of a girl but you are every inch a woman. You are mine, and no matter what, my Bliss, you will remain so—even if you hate me.'

'Hate you?' Her arms had looped themselves about his neck and she could feel the heat and exciting readiness of his strong body against hers. 'I could never do that to you, Paris.'

'You say so, *moiya*, but everything is possible where you and I are concerned,' and even as he spoke he possessed her and time slid off the edge of the universe; they were alone and together and Bliss felt as if she held all the force of life between her two encircling arms.

The rapture between them was more potent than ever, for her body was no longer a novice to the joys it could be made to feel. And Paris was so passionately desirous, so enabled to take her from one sensation to another until they cascaded through the very marrow of her being.

The sun was going down when the joy of it culminated and as the fiery rays burned across the balcony into the bedroom, Paris seemed a brazen figure there against her whiteness, his face at rest in her tousled hair.

'You smell like wheat which has felt the sun upon it from sunrise to sunfall,' he murmured. 'You are my field of golden surprises, *pedhaki mou*.'

'Why do I surprise you, Paris?' The tips of her

breasts were at rest in the warm hair of his chest, and her legs lay curled about his. She felt a sensual relaxation that was exquisite, and a kind of animal joy in her discovery of her own body, so that being close like this to the body of her lover was the most profound experience she would ever know.

'You are as passionate as any Greek woman,' he replied.

'Is that a compliment, Paris, or a confession?' She spoke teasingly, but at the same time she had become curious about the women he must have known, and lain with in the aftermath of physical pleasure. 'Have you had lots of women in your life?'

'I wasn't always married,' he mocked her. 'And my mother did not give birth to a son with the inclinations of a celibate. There were women I liked and admired—it wasn't until I saw you, *moiya*, that I felt like giving up my freedom.'

'It's strange,' she murmured, 'but I hated the thought of being tied to a man. When I used to ride across the moors, all bronze and purple, a sparkle on the streams like polished armour, I wanted never to belong to anything or anyone that took away my free spirit. I even preferred to ride bareback so my horse could feel as free as I.

'As I said, *pedhaki mou*, you never led me to believe that I could possess you so utterly.' He raised himself and studied her face in the tawny-red light filling the room. 'Do you fully realise how completely you gave yourself to me?'

She smiled into his eyes and raised a hand to his face, pressing it to his hardened cheek. 'Being with you is like riding wild and free on the moors—there is something of their untameable quality in you, Paris. Something of their rocky mystery that lays a spell upon the spirit. Paris, when will we go to Cathlamet?'

A silence hung upon her words, and then he drew away from her and stood up, a tall figure in the waning light. Something seemed to brush against Bliss's heart, a small finger that left an ache in its wake.

'What is it, Paris?' She sat up, straining with wide eyes to read the expression on his face, but his face was masked by the shadows that were creeping into the room, dispelling the warm fire of the sun, gone down into the sea.

'Paris?'

'We are here on Dovima to enjoy our honeymoon,' he said, almost sombrely. 'Can't you forget Cathlamet for a while?'

'Yes—if you don't ask me to forget it altogether.' She kneeled in almost a supplicating way. 'Don't ask me to wrench Cathlamet out of my heart—I'd hoped that we were going to make our home there.'

'We shall see!' He turned on his heel with the words, snatched up his discarded clothes and walked off into the adjoining room. As the door closed, Bliss sought her robe and walked out barefoot on to the balcony, its stonework and iron cooling after the heat of the sun.

She leaned on the railing and listened to the distant splash of the sea. Overhead the stars were flooding the purple-dark sky and the air smelled of the resin drifting from the pinewoods that clothed the island.

She could bear it if Paris wanted her to live part of the time in his beloved Greece; his mother lived here and it was understandable if he wanted to be with her.

What Bliss couldn't endure was the thought of never spending time at Cathlamet, whose gracious old image was always with her. She not only loved its felicitous honey-coloured stone, but its every nook and cranny was imprinted upon her memory. Her bedroom there, with the walls panelled in a paper that was vivid with birds and branches and delicately shaded leaves. There was a Chippendale bed with the canopy raised upon slender carved posts, the fabric of the canopy matching the wallpaper, and lined at the back of the bed with sky-blue silk matching the counterpane.

A pair of lovely old Persian carpets were spread upon the honey-toned timber floor, and there was a bedside cabinet where she had kept her books, and a side-table where her collection of fans in silk and lace were always spread out.

The gallery was rich with Grinling Gibbons carvings of wheatsheafs, pigeons and flower petals, all beautifully detailed. And there were Grinling Gibbons door fittings with their graceful carving, and the magical coloured dome of the conservatory opening out from the morning-room.

A great grass court fronted the house and great floods of sunlight came through the deeply recessed windows, making mullioned patterns all over the floor.

How well remembered the beautiful oak floor

and benches of the hall, and the tapestry work of the chair seats. How warming that huge fireplace of black Irish marble where the big logs were burned, their skins crackling with the heat.

How much she loved that extravagant and romantic skyline of gables and curving turrets, while her most favoured room of all had been the Peacock Room, so called because of the painted ceiling of a lustrous peacock with azure feathers showing the eye.

Bliss loved Cathlamet as Paris loved Greece, and her instincts were warning her that their harmony of body was not going to find its reflection in their desires of the heart. Nothing could change the fact that he was Greek and she was English, and that both of them were as strong-willed as their passions.

Not until her union with Paris had Bliss realised the breadth of her own passions, and though the very thought of being in his arms was enough to make her legs feel weak, she was set on fighting him if he denied her the pleasure of living now and then at Cathlamet.

Being Greek, it was inherent in him to be the dominant partner in their marriage, and Bliss had no intention of being other than his woman, but it was inherent in her to feel the pull of the old Yorkstone house where generations of the St Cyr family had spent their lives, and now she was married to Paris the house was hers to see again.

A cool breeze blew upwards off the sea and played with her hair as she stood there lost in her thoughts. First she could cajole him, but if he proved adamant about their residence in Greece, then she was prepared to lose her temper. He had compared her to a Greek woman, and she was quite certain that they were as tempered as the men, and if that didn't work then she'd break down in tears.

Bliss smiled to herself ... there was really quite a bit of fun and drama in being married, for no matter how strong and demanding the man, ultimately he was at the mercy of a woman's vulnerability. It was something a man couldn't help but be aware of when he held a woman in his arms. He was aware of her breakability, aware of how easily he could bruise her softer skin and her more sensitive emotions.

She broke into a little, almost anticipatory laugh and returned to the bedroom where she carefully straightened and smoothed the sheets and plumped the pillows. In a while Aspasia would come to run her bath and lay out her evening dress, and there was something about the woman that gave Bliss an edgy feeling.

The Greek woman didn't like her, and Bliss didn't like it that Aspasia was privy to her intimacy with Paris. It was like having a spy in her bedroom, for Bliss was quite convinced that Aspasia was watching her every move in order to report on the honeymoon to Madame Apollonaris.

Bliss eyed the much tidier bed and told herself that one thing was certain, Aspasia couldn't inform Paris's mother that his bride was a reluctant one. It was quite evident that her son was receiving a great deal of affectionate response from his English wife, and that might have been her concern. She would know her son better than anyone else and would want for him a wife who would welcome all that passionate power in Paris; all that need to assuage the long-ago hurts and rejections of his boyhood.

Bliss settled the coverlet so it was perfectly cornered, and with a catch of her breath remembered how deliriously happy she had been in her husband's powerful arms, carried away in them to throbbing heights of pleasure, almost maddened by his hands upon her, by his sensuous kisses that made her cry out and cleave to his lean and muscular body.

As memory swept her, she sank down on the tidied bed and wrapped her arms about her body, where within the pleasure centres of herself the glow had not yet waned. Her heart beat fast and her senses swam just to think of the intimate secrets she had shared with Paris. The tips of her fingers still tingled from being in contact with him, and she could feel the tips of her breasts alive and aware against the silkiness of her robe.

Oh God—she was swept from head to toe by a yearning that brought the tears into her eyes. Paris possessed her even when he was apart from her. His dark Greek image filled her mind just as his kisses and caresses lingered upon her skin, and suddenly she was weeping with the joy his hard, strong body had left within her.

'The *kyria* is sad?'

Bliss glanced up startled into the watchful eyes of Aspasia, a few tears still spilling down her cheeks. 'Why—no.'

'The *kyria* weeps, so she must be in a sad mood.'

'My mood isn't at all sad.' Bliss stood up, noticing how Aspasia's eyes roamed over the bed.

'The *kyria* should not have bothered to tidy the bed.' Aspasia's eyes were dark and sharp. 'It is my task to do so.'

'Your task is not to be so presumptuous!' Suddenly her distrust of the woman had made Bliss lose her temper. 'Please run me a bath and add the pine crystals—and tell me something! Has Madame Apollonaris left orders that I'm to be watched by you and my every movement made the subject of a report?'

But Aspasia was wily and she at once gave Bliss a blank look. 'I do not understand the *kyria* when she speaks so quickly in English.'

'You understand me well enough—please run my bath.'

'*Ne*, madame.'

Directly Aspasia entered the bathroom Bliss went to the alcoved cupboard and selected the dress she would wear for dinner with Paris; that darned snooping woman wasn't going to presume to do the selection, or a few more sparks would fly! The dress was a simple opalescent silk chiffon with sheer lantern sleeves, and Bliss chose a pair of silver shoes to wear with it—shoes, of course, which she had worn last evening when she had fled away from Paris through his garden of stone figures.

So short a time ago, and yet it seemed a misty memory. Had she really felt such fear of him? She smiled as she pinned up her hair so the ends wouldn't become straggly and wet while she bathed, then she waited for Aspasia to come out of the bathroom and casually requested that a pot of tea be brought to her.

'Just tell the cook not to put the tea into the pot with a tablespoon,' she smiled airly. 'Just two teaspoonfuls will do nicely, and the pot need only be half filled with boiling water. Understood?'

'*Ne*, madame.' Aspasia left the bedroom politely enough, but Bliss was aware of her resentment. She was the type who liked to be privy to her mistress's secrets, and she most certainly didn't like it that she was being foiled by Bliss. If, as Bliss suspected, she was spying for Madame Apollonaris, then it might be as well to tell Paris. He, no more than Bliss, would want his mother to be told resentful things about her.

Bliss indulged in a pine-scented bath which left her skin tingling and fresh, then she re-entered the bedroom in her robe, quickly enough to catch Aspasia holding aloft the silk chiffon dress and halfway to the alcoved cupboard with it.

'What are you doing?' she demanded.

Aspasia turned and faced her, her dark eyes defiant. 'The *kyria* has beautiful dresses of *haute couture* which the master has bought her, so she should wear them to please him. A Greek woman lives only to please her husband.'

'What a lot of rubbish!' Bliss marched across the room and held out her hand for the silk chiffon. 'I'm new to the Greek climate and I wish to feel cool, so please hand me my dress or I shall call in the *kyrios* and have you dismissed this instant!'

'The *kyrios* would not dismiss me because I am in the service of his mother.' Aspasia flicked her eyes up and down Bliss in her casually tied robe, with her hair still pinned to the crown of her head. 'The English cannot understand the loyalties of the Greeks.'

'I understand very well the bond between my husband and his mother,' Bliss rejoined, feeling her nerves tightening into little knots. 'But I warn you not to run away with the idea that he would put his mother's wishes before mine.'

'Merely because of—that!' Aspasia flung out a hand towards the bed. 'You think you are the first woman in the *kyrios's* life?'

'I am the first wife in his life!' Bliss reached out to take her dress and instantly Aspasia jerked it away, pulling it so quickly free of Bliss's fingers that the material ripped, the fine chiffon tearing away from the silk.

For an instant Aspasia looked afraid, then defiantly she thrust the torn dress at Bliss. 'You did it, madame! You cannot put the blame on me— you tried to snatch the dress in your temper!'

Bliss stood holding the dress as Aspasia dashed from the room, and only half a minute later Paris entered through the gaping door. 'Have you had words with the maid?' he asked. 'She fled past me in tears, mumbling something about a torn dress you were blaming on her—ah, is that the offending garment?'

He strolled across the room until he loomed over Bliss, who was in the grip of nervous anger at the way Aspasia had put her in the wrong. She met Paris's enquiring, slightly amused eyes and instantly decided that she didn't want to spoil his mood of well-being.

'I—I don't seem to be getting on very well with your mother's maid.' She forced herself to speak lightly. 'She wanted me to wear one of my grand dresses and we had a bit of an argument— I'm beginning to realise just how self-willed you Greek people are.'

'I'm afraid my mother is inclined to let Aspasia have her own way.' Paris took hold of the torn dress and examined it. 'A pity, it's a pretty thing. However, you have other dresses and I daresay a woman on the island can be found who will mend the garment.'

Bliss realised that the situation struck Paris as fairly frivolous, and once again she decided that this wasn't the moment to impart her suspicion that she was being deliberately spied upon and made to feel an intrusive foreigner.

As she went over to select another dress, Paris sat down in one of the armchairs and was obviously going to be her audience while she put it on. A smile quivered on her lips as she withdrew a dress of smoky satin, with a mandarin collar and long slim lines. She was bare beneath her robe and she wondered just how hungry he was for his dinner, if he was going to watch her through those dark lashes as she put on her underwear.

Saturnine and distinguished in his dinner suit and white ruffled shirt, Paris quietly, absorbedly watched as Bliss slid a silken slip down over the curves of her body; as with a shyness she had to control she stepped into silky matching panties.

'Are you enjoying this one-woman show?' she murmured, as she went to the mirror to unpin and comb her hair. She could see him through the glass, the side of his mouth dented by a smile.

'It's my privilege,' he said, with a touch of arrogance. 'You are mine from head to heel, are you not?'

'What a possessive devil you are, Paris.' She slid a mother-of-pearl clip into the left side of her smooth hair, leaving the right side to curve freely against her cheekbone. With a light hand she made up her face, applying a rose colour to her lips and lightly spraying her skin with *eau-de-rose*.

Paris still watched her in that lazily intent way as she clad her slim legs in sheer hose and stepped into her silver shoes . . . it was as she was reaching for the smoky satin dress that he came to his feet and with a pantherish stride came and stood behind her, his hands clasping her silk-clad hips, his lips seeking the side of her neck so she was made helpless by her need to submit to his touch.

'From head to heel I have made you mine,' he breathed against her scented skin. 'If you went a thousand miles from me . . . if you went to the other side of the world, still you would know that you belong to me.'

'Why should I ever want to leave you?' She felt the responsive quiver of her skin to the caress of his lips. 'I'm happy to stay.'

'Take care of certain words, Bliss, for we Greeks try not to challenge the fates by proclaiming aloud our joy. I personally abide by the decree of Apollo, that a man should live as though he had only one more day to enjoy the sunlight.'

'You fatalist,' she taunted softly. 'You are so worldly in some ways, Paris, but so primitive in others.'

'You bring out the primitive in me, and you revel in doing so, eh?'

Yes, her heart responded. She was incredibly excited by that streak of the untamed in Paris, even though warned that it would be dangerous to set it loose in anger.

'Right now I'm fearfully hungry for my dinner,' she rejoined, 'so I'll refrain from any revels until we've eaten.'

He laughed deeply, laid a kiss at the side of her neck and drew his hands away from her body. 'Shall I be your valet and help you into your dress?'

She nodded, and felt a certain tenderness in him as he enclosed her in the smoke-coloured dress, a sheath of satin that reflected the colour of her eyes. At the pool of her throat, where the mandarin collar was slit, the ruby heart glowed on its golden chain.

'Such lovely eyes,' he cradled her face in his hands, 'like moonwater.'

'My husband, the primitive poet,' she smiled up at him. 'Are you really Apollo, I wonder?'

He shook his head and his eyes slowly narrowed until they were fiery and dangerous. 'Apollo of the sun was pure Greek, but I have Turkish blood in my veins; shades of the warrior and the *seraglio* are there in my attitude towards you, and you know it, don't you, Bliss?'

'Yes,' her heart beat fast, as the heart does on the crest of joy or fear, 'I knew it when we first met, yet I'm here with you, Paris ... you had your way and I married you.'

'The British were always brave,' he smiled, and arm linked in arm they went down to dinner.

CHAPTER ELEVEN

THEY dined in the attractive white and gold, *saloni*, and the meal they ate was purely Greek, the first course being *dolmathes*, which were delicious rolls of minced meat, rice and herbs wrapped in tender vine leaves. A slightly heady Greek wine was served with them, adding to their savoury flavour.

'Good?' Paris watched Bliss as she ate, the candle flames reflecting in his eyes as he faced her across the round table in a deep alcove where the windows stood open to let in the cool and tangy air.

'Mmm, I'm so hungry! It must be the island air.'

'The air, among other things.' His eyes held a gleam of devilry as he raised his wine glass and savoured the wine. 'Did you know that Greek islands are encircled by deep-down rocks that create a ring of silver when seen from the air?'

'Is that why you like islands, Paris, because in a way they symbolise your own nature?'

'You think I have rocks deep in my nature, Bliss?'

'I know you have,' she said simply. 'I would never make the mistake of thinking that all is smooth sailing where you're concerned, Paris. You'd be a less fascinating man if you were shallow and had no rocky depths. You pulled yourself up from rock bottom to become a man of property, didn't you?'

'And you admire me for that, *pedhi mou*.'

'Most women admire strength and grit and the self-discipline that goes with attainment.' She smiled into his eyes across the rim of her wine glass. 'You're also ruthless, of course, but I'll forgive you for that.'

'Magnanimous of you, my dear, but what if I had to be ruthless with you?'

'In what way, Paris?' She felt her heartbeat quicken and sensed that the image of Cathlamet was taking shape in the air between them. Soon ... very soon they must discuss its place in their lives, but she wouldn't spoil their dinner by broaching the matter right now. There was time enough, and she didn't want to shatter their mood of harmony, lingering from their afternoon of love.

'In the most obvious way, *moiya*. I am Greek and you are British, and inevitably we shall pull in opposite directions. In some matters I shall give in to you because you are so physically appealing to me that I enjoy indulging you.'

'I am to be allowed small victories, but you are going to reserve the big ones for yourself, is that it, Paris?'

'I intend to be the master in my own home,' he agreed. 'Would you have me otherwise, Bliss? Would you continue to admire my strength of character if I turned into a weak man dominated by a woman intent on having all her own way?'

'I could never dominate you.' Bliss laughed at the mere idea, for the very look of Paris ruled out such a hope even if she had harboured one. Power was stamped into his features, and early hard work had packed strength and endurance into his body. Being physically close to him hadn't ruled out the touch of fear that he engendered in her.

A close acquaintance with his body hadn't given her access to his mind and still in many ways he was the stranger from a foreign land who had taken control of her life much as he had taken possession of Cathlamet. The overriding difference was that he seemed indifferent to the house, which was natural enough, she supposed, for who could expect a Greek to find an old stone mansion on the Yorkshire moors of any great interest?

Their meal continued with crisply roasted lamb and a selection of succulent vegetables in a delicious gravy. The wine was changed to a slightly richer one, and Bliss reflected that by the end of dinner she would be more than a little intoxicated.

As she pushed her wine glass away she saw Paris draw his brows together in a frown.

'Is the wine not to your taste?' he asked.

'It's a little too tasty,' she smiled. 'I'm not really a good drinker; too much wine goes to my head.'

'If you can't walk upstairs to bed, then I shall carry you. Come, lift your glass and drink with me—I insist!'

'Paris, are you trying to intoxicate me?'

'I want you to feel carefree, that is all. We are on honeymoon and every moment should be savoured; there should be no shadow to spoil our time together, just as there is no speck to spoil the clarity of this wine, which has been distilled from the wild grapes of Dovima.'

'Very well,' Bliss sipped from her glass, 'how can I refuse you when you turn on your Greek charisma?'

'So you know it to be a Greek word?'

'I looked it up in the dictionary and learned that it has a Greek derivation meaning supernatural power and talent . . . you do have those qualities, don't you, Paris?'

'Do I?' He smiled obliquely. 'You will have to learn my language, Bliss, for its roots are entangled with your own. There is a remarkable teacher of languages in Athens from whom I learned English, and I think it would be to your advantage to take lessons from him. You would like to enrol with him?'

'Paris,' she swallowed deeply of her wine, for she needed the courage, 'are you saying that when we leave Dovima we're going to live in Athens?'

'I have a large apartment there, so it would seem the natural thing to do.' He deliberately cut into the crisp slice of lamb on his plate. 'You have objections to my plan?'

'I had hoped,' she took a deep breath, 'I dreamed that we might make Cathlamet our home—at least for part of the year! Mayn't we?'

He ate with deliberation, almost as if hesitant to answer her question.

'Paris, please say yes!' Her eyes were fixed upon him, the man who had held her in his arms

all the afternoon, who couldn't be cruel enough
to say that living at Cathlamet was an impossible
dream which she must put out of her mind.

'I suggest that we discuss the matter over
coffee,' he said. 'Let us first enjoy our dessert,
eh?'

'Am I unlikely to enjoy your decision on
Cathlamet?' Bliss tried to speak composedly, but
her voice shook. She could hardly bear to face
what was going to happen in a very short while;
his manner warned her that all the lovely
harmony they had discovered together was going
to hit discordant notes when it came to
Cathlamet. What would she do, how would she
react if he was going to tell her that he'd decided
to sell the house?

Their dessert came to the table, and though it
was a delectable flan of hot spicy fruits covered in
chilled cream, Bliss had lost her appetite and was
aware of Paris watching her as she forced herself
to eat a small section of the flan.

He didn't chide her, nor did he speak until
they entered the *zala* where coffee was brought to
them. He stood with his coffee cup and saucer in
hand, and she was intensely aware of the resolute
power in his tall figure outlined against the white
wall, beneath the deep blue ceiling where a great
bell of a chandelier hung. The carpet was of
astrakhan and circular, and on the deep sill of the
wide window stood vases of black pottery inlaid
with white Grecian patterns.

Somewhere beyond the windows there was a
sound of Greek music beating through the still
night air, inseparable notes of joy and sorrow that

made the music more tantalising than anything Bliss had ever heard.

It seemed to be telling her that life with a Greek was never a compromise, it was Arcadia where shadows lurked, producing zest and suffering in equal measure.

She set aside her coffee cup and pushed nervous fingers through her hair, which like a silky veil half concealed her face from him. She was nerving herself to speak, searching for words that wouldn't lead her into an argument with him, when he spoke in the deep and deliberate voice that could so disarm her.

'I have been trying to find an apt way to describe your hair, *moiya*, and it comes to me that it's like the silver that flashes on the underwing of a hawk in flight.'

Beyond the windows the music beat like a metallic heart and the pine trees were alive with a chorus of cicadas. As Bliss swung her legs beneath her, there on the low couch, her dress shimmered like smoke about her body and she cast hunted eyes around this room with its ivory-white carpet, its lamps on white onyx bases, and its hand-carved furniture. Her gaze finally rested on a niche in which stood an ivory ikon with a half-masked head.

Her nerves seemed to leap against her skin when a lighter clicked and a cloud of cigar smoke drifted towards her.

'Speak your thought, Bliss,' he ordered. 'We have had coffee and I promised you an answer to your question about Cathlamet.'

Without shifting her gaze from the ikon Bliss

asked him again if they might spend part of their year at Cathlamet.

'There is no possibility of it, I'm afraid.'

His reply stunned her, for it seemed so cruel and heartless. Her eyes flashed to his face, hurt and bewildered, and through the wreathing smoke his features seemed as if cast in bronze . . . to match his hard heart, she told herself wildly.

'You're not afraid,' she flung at him. 'People need hearts in order to feel anything, and you're so up to your neck in armour that you couldn't care less about stabbing me!'

In an extremity of hurt she kneeled on the couch and appealed to him with her hands stretched out. 'Why are you so opposed to us spending time there—you know how much I care about Cathlamet! It broke my heart when I found out that my father couldn't support it any more— why, Paris, why didn't you sell it right away if you never meant to live there? Did you hold on to it—like an ace up your sleeve—as another means of getting me to marry you? Is that all Cathlamet meant to you?'

He smoked in silence for about half a minute, his gaze fixed upon her anguished face in the frame of her silvery hair. Then abruptly he plunged a hand into the pocket of his dinner jacket and produced an envelope. A couple of strides brought him to the side of the couch, where he paused, then handed her the envelope.

'You had better take a look at this, child.'

Her hands felt nerveless as she took the envelope and looked inside; she withdrew what was obviously a Telex communication and opened it. It was printed in Greek, but one word stood out and as she read it she spoke it.

'Cathlamet!'

Her gaze went swiftly to the smoke-wreathed face above her. 'What does it mean, Paris? What does the message say?'

'Before I tell you, Bliss, I suggest that you have a little brandy.' Cigar clenched between his teeth, Paris went to a side-table and the clink of the glasses made the only sound as he poured brandy for both of them, the only outward sign that he was disturbed by what he had to translate.

Bliss accepted her brandy glass with her left hand, the Telex still clenched in the fingers of her right hand. 'Tell me,' she breathed, and in her anxiety the bones of her face were clearly defined, tiny featherings of shadow beneath her cheekbones.

Paris stared down at her and he made no attempt to take the Telex from her grip. 'I know the words by heart,' he said. 'It states that Cathlamet had been engulfed by a fire . . . there is very little of the house left standing.'

She took in the words, she suffered their meaning, but they made no sense. Cathlamet had been part of her existence since the day she was born. In winter and summer, in all the seasons, it had stood strong and indestructible on the moors, there above the village of Wychley, where the road wended its way down to the Belt of Oaks, the old local inn among the stone-fronted houses all joined together but with their slate roofs at different levels. Hard shiny slate and the local stone that weathered so well. Some of the house walls were cobbled and the contrast was picturesque. The road itself was of smooth flat stones and the pavement was a narrow track. There was an old Norman church of dark stone, with shops built into its cobbled walls, and the quaint old inn had greenery and roses against its whitened walls, with mullioned windows sloping out, black chains looped on posts along its frontage.

So many times had she walked down in the late afternoon sun, then back again across Hedda's Moor, past the old weaving house, with its diamond-paned windows and board-clad walls. Marigolds grew in the yard and every summer she had plucked a handful to take home with her because the gardener at Cathlamet refused to let them grow along his borders.

'No——' She shook her head in disbelief. 'How can Cathlamet be burned?'

Paris sat down beside her, stubbing his cigar as he did so. 'Come, drink your brandy, *moiya*, it will assist you in feeling a little better.'

But in her thoughts she was far from Paris in this moment, and wandering again through the house where she had spent all her early years. How could all that rich honey-coloured oak be in ashes, along with the casement windows with the stained glass that depicted legendary soldiers and lovers with the St Cyr name? How could the marquetry-work be gone, and the antique benches in their oak frames? She couldn't believe that those tall panelled doors would no longer open upon the graceful rooms, where ivory brocade hung at the windows and where high-shouldered leather chairs stood ready to be occupied.

'It can't be true?' Her eyes implored his denial, but instead he put his own brandy glass to her lips and his eyes commanded her to drink.

She did so, choking a little against the strength of the brandy, warmed by his hands.

'The house is gutted,' he said, his eyes holding hers. 'There are, I'm informed, only a few walls left standing . . . exterior walls.'

Bliss shuddered. 'L-like stone memorials!'

'I'm afraid so, Bliss.' Once again he urged her to swallow some brandy and she did so, having to make an effort to get it past the lump that was forming in her throat. 'W-when did it happen, Paris? How did it happen?'

He explained that decorating materials, such as paints and oily rags, were believed to have caused the fire in conjunction with a cigarette which had, perhaps, been left burning in the room where the materials were kept.

'The insurance company will discover the exact cause.' Paris abruptly tossed back his own brandy, his fingers tight around the bowl.

As the shock of the news spread through Bliss she studied the Telex, her eyes fixed upon the one word which she understood, the name of the house that a careless painter had reduced to only a few outside walls. As an image of the blaze spread through her mind she shuddered forcibly.

'When did you receive—this?' She gave Paris a sad look. 'Was it brought across on the caique with your mail?'

He seemed to hesitate, then he set his jaw so

that it looked iron hard. 'It was received at my hotel on the morning of our marriage.'

Bliss absorbed his words, then their meaning, and suddenly it was as if a spark set a fire smouldering within her. 'Why didn't you tell me? I had a right to be told!'

'I was concerned——'

'What concerned you, Paris?' She fixed her eyes upon his face. 'Did you think I'd run out on our marriage?'

'There was a possibility of it,' he admitted. 'I am aware that Cathlamet was one of the reasons why you married me.'

'I—I'm glad you're aware of it.' All at once Bliss needed a target for her shocking sense of loss; her anger and despair at having to visualise Cathlamet as a smoke-blackened ruin rather than a gracious landmark which had stood upon the moors for centuries.

This hurt that she felt bore no relation to her indignation when the house had fallen into Paris's hands . . . then he had been a dark stranger, but now he was closer to her than anyone had ever been and he hadn't trusted her enough on their wedding day to share with her the tragedy of Cathlamet.

He had stood beside her at the altar table in the Greek church, and she felt quite certain that all through the ceremony the Telex had been hidden away in the pocket of his suit.

'Yes,' she said, in a cold voice, 'I'd have had no reason left to marry you, Paris. My brother was out of your reach, and you knew very well that had you shown me the Telex, then I certainly

wouldn't have been in the mood to marry you.
That would have upset all your plans, wouldn't
it? Your mother and your friends wouldn't have
understood why your English fiancée should be
upset over the destruction of a centuries-old
house——'

'Stop this, Bliss!' He reached out to touch her
and in a flare of temper she flung his hand away.

'All you were thinking about was your Greek
pride—your precious sense of *philotemo*! Self-
respect, holding your head high, loving your own
honour—those are what matter to you, aren't
they, Paris?'

'They matter,' he agreed, 'but I didn't see what
there was to be gained by spoiling the day for
everyone. I knew very well that the house meant
a lot to you, but ultimately we all grow up, Bliss,
and it was time for you to become my wife, to live
your life in conjunction with mine, and though it
was tragic that Cathlamet should perish in
flames, I also felt that in the strangest way it was
decreed by the fates.'

Bliss stared at him, and his words were fuel
upon the anger that was smouldering inside her,
showing its smoke in her blazing eyes. 'I suppose
you didn't have it burned down on purpose?' she
cried out.

He caught his breath harshly and the knuckles
of his right hand showed like bone against the
cut-glass of the brandy bowl which he still held
... the silence was broken as the bowl suddenly
toppled from the base, snapped in his grip. He
released the stem and it fell to the carpet with the
broken bowl.

'How dare you say such a thing to me!'

For an instant Bliss was frightened by the look on his face, but she strove not to cower away from him. 'Can you blame me for thinking it?' she asked defiantly. 'It would be one way for you to keep me here in Greece.'

'The fire that destroyed Cathlamet was not deliberate.' Still his brows cast a dark and thundery look over his face. 'Redecorating was in progess because I fully intended for us to enjoy the house whenever it was possible for me to spend time in England. I took it for granted that you understood that the bulk of my business commitments are here in my own country ... there was never any way that we could make our home permanently at Cathlamet, but it would have been our holiday home, and that is the truth.'

A sense of justice told Bliss that she was hearing the truth, but it didn't soothe her feelings or bank down the angry sense of injustice that he had knowledge of the fire while she had been kept in ignorance of it.

'Y-you had no right not to tell me,' she said, and because on the couch he was too close to her she rose to her feet and walked away from him. 'I was born there, Paris. I grew up at Cathlamet and loved every nook and cranny of it, inside and out. How the sight of it burning must have awed and frightened the villagers—oh God, I can hardly bear to think of it!'

As she sank her face in her hands Paris stood up and came to her, but for the moment he made no second attempt to try and touch her. 'Perhaps

I did wrong, Bliss, in not telling you, but in all sincerity I had my reasons. Also we Greeks have a proverb, "There are some things so dangerous they must not be spoken," and that was how it was for me on the morning when we were to be joined together as man and wife.'

He drew a deep, audible breath, as of a man about to dive into even deeper depths. 'Receiving the news that morning was like an omen and I had to ignore it. It was something too dangerous to speak of, and I had to wait until it was safe to do so.'

'Safe?' Bliss uncovered her face and made herself look at him. 'What do you mean by safe, Paris? When you had me here on your island and after you'd made sure of me in bed?'

'Ah, Bliss,' he almost groaned her name, 'that is no way to speak of it.'

'Of our *nuit d'amour*?' she asked cynically. 'I don't think the destruction of Cathlamet was on your conscience for one moment of that night. You had once again achieved one of your goals, and that is what your life is dedicated to, isn't it, Paris? Come what may, you will retaliate for all the snubs you received as a child. You will go on showing everyone that you have made it from rags to riches and in the process taken for your wife the daughter of a man you helped to bankrupt.'

'By hell, that isn't true!' He glowered down at her, suddenly a man in bare control of his emotions. 'Your father was an insatiable gambler, driven to destroy not only himself but those he should have cared for beyond his own indulgences. He piled up debts at the Club Cassandra, and when at last I refused to support them, he went elsewhere, until there wasn't a stone, a brick or a slate of Cathlamet that wasn't gambled away. I repossessed the title deeds from the person who had them, and the day you and I met at Cathlamet was possibly a fatal one.'

Paris paused and thrust a hand through his black hair, again and yet again until it was dishevelled. 'Yes, *moiya*, I saw you for the first time; you were in a paddock nearby the house and you were training a young horse, holding him on a long bridle, a dark-coated colt walking in wide circles around your own fair and slender figure. You didn't notice me just then, for you were absorbed in what you were doing. I entered your home with the intention of returning those Cathlamet deeds, but your father had been drinking and I could see that yet again your home would fall into the hands of a club owner——

'Ah yes, I am the owner of a club, Bliss, but I have my standards even if you choose to believe otherwise. And it's quite true that when you and I came face to face in the hall of Cathlamet I was the master of the house instead of your father. From that moment onward you were supported by me—but not because it gave me satisfaction in the sense of crowing over an English gentleman who had fallen on his face! I despised his lack of character, but I didn't enjoy seeing his deterioration, and I was determined that your life wasn't going to be spoiled because of him!'

'How gallant of you, Paris.'

They faced each other again . . . and again in a

house of which he was the master. Bliss felt a wave of misery and loss sweep over her ... there seemed nothing left that she could claim for her own ... all she was, all she had ever been, was the bride which Paris had bought for himself.

Misery can culminate in tears, or produce a need to express itself more violently.

She looked at Paris and his face had never looked so closed to her, as if all the muscles were of iron. She saw no sympathy there for the death of Cathlamet, and all at once she seemed to fling herself forward on her toes and her hand swung twice against his face, leaving imprints that were plain to see upon the flesh that wasn't iron after all.

'You think your money can buy everything ... make up for losing the things that matter! Cathlamet mattered to me, a-and you stand there looking as if a—a cowshed has burned down instead of m-my home!'

'Your home?' he echoed. 'You told me in London that when the house fell into my hands you no longer considered it part of your life.'

'That was before I——' She bit down on the word so hard that she almost broke the skin of her lip.

'Before you married me,' he said, looking ironic. 'But when you became my wife the great and wonderful house was once again of prime importance to you—by heaven, what a child you can be! Have you learned nothing about life in the hours we've spent together?'

'Yes,' she said defiantly, 'I've learned that all you really want is the shape of me! You don't care a hoot in hell that I—I'm suffering because of what has happened to Cathlamet!'

'Of course I care when you suffer——'

'In case it damages the goods?' she asked, using the kind of words she normally regarded as slangy and cheap. 'You paid a high price for me, didn't you Paris? You're bound to want value for your money, so in terms of *drachmae* you must be fuming about the loss of Cathlamet.'

'Yes, I'm fuming right now.' His teeth showed hard and white, and when he took a sudden step towards her Bliss felt a lurch of panic inside her, realising some of the things she had said to him. Well, he had deserved them, she told herself as she backed away from him. He was being quite heartless about the beautiful old house where a few scorched walls stood in memory of all the memories which had been stored up in Cathlamet.

Her heart ached unbearably and there was no comfort to be found in the stony-faced man who watched her so intently . . . looking as if her love of the destroyed house made him angry instead of sympathetic.

'Perhaps if you had my memories of a house you grew up in you might be more understanding,' she said recklessly. 'But you grew up in a field, didn't you, and that would make a difference!'

A silence followed her words . . . an appalled silence that Bliss had to shatter with more reckless words, or run from. She chose to run!

CHAPTER TWELVE

SNATCHING the long skirt of her dress above her ankles, Bliss fled across the hall, where the keystone of welcome lay beneath her running feet. To the tempestuous beat of her heart she ran upstairs, and it wasn't until she reached her room that emotion clutched at the very inside of her and she sank down against the side of the bed, racked by sobs.

All the fight ran out of her with the scalding tears, and when at last she struggled to her feet she felt drained of strength as well.

It was an actual effort to relieve herself of her dress, and tiredly she stepped out of the satin pool and went into the bathroom to wash her tear-stained face.

She felt as if she had wept for all the sad things in her life, as if they had been stored up inside her waiting to be released. She was free now of all the obligations pertaining to Cathlamet. On its pyre all her debts had been repaid, and she knew exactly what she was going to do when morning came.

When she re-entered the bedroom she found that a tray had been brought to her, on which stood a pot of tea, a cup and saucer, cream and sugar and custard cream biscuits.

Shivering slightly in her robe, she poured herself a cup of tea and sweetened it strongly.

The hot tea helped to dispel some of the shock she had received, and she sat in an armchair near the window, eyes still smarting from that flood of tears, as far as possible from the chair in which Paris had lounged, enjoying his ownership of her. That was all she meant to him, something to own ... something he liked to see in satin and lace, pleasing his eye and his passions!

Her eyes stung with tears again and she fought them back, taking deep gulps of tea in an effort to stem the tide of misery. She firmly told herself that she had wept enough for one night and now she must decide on a plan of action with regard to getting away from the island.

Asking Paris to release her in a civilised manner would be pointless. It would only alert him to what she had in mind, and though it might enter his head that she would make an effort to run away from him, he would assume that the loyalty of his staff would make it impossible for her to leave Dovima, there being only one way to leave, and that was in a boat.

But Bliss had an ace up her sleeve, a term she had often heard Justin use. She was aware of Aspasia's resentment of her and was glad that she hadn't mentioned to Paris her suspicion that his mother's maid was spying on her, watching her as a cat watches a mouse so she could cause mischief.

Bliss would provide her with ample mischief, and after finishing her tea she set about packing a few necessary items in readiness for her departure, folding a change of underwear and a blouse into a handbag and making sure she had money in her purse. She hid the handbag away in the clothes closet, then quietly opened her bedroom door.

No one was about; she had felt instinctively that Paris would leave her alone to weep or sulk, but instead she made her way to Aspasia's room on the floor above the main gallery.

Quietly but firmly she tapped on the door of the maid's bedroom, and after a few moments it opened and Aspasia stood there, tying the sash of her robe. Her dark hair was undone and it made a flowing cape about her shoulders, while the carnation-pink of her robe made her seem softer and more friendly.

But Bliss wasn't fooled ... she had been confronted by the real Aspasia earlier in the evening and she was quite certain that if she was to succeed in getting away from Dovima, then this was the person to approach.

'You want something, madame?'

'Yes—may I come in? I don't want to be seen.'

In an instant Aspasia's eyes sharpened and she widened the door so Bliss could enter, then closed it and stood with her back to it, her enquiring gaze fixed upon her mistress.

'I want to be taken to the mainland in the morning,' Bliss had decided to be blunt and matter-of-fact about it. 'Can you find someone who will take me? I have money, so I can pay for the trip.'

Aspasia gave no outward sign that she was amazed by the request, and she certainly didn't look dismayed. Her dark eyes moved up and down Bliss's figure, clad in a negligee of peachy silk, a garment from the trousseau which Paris had paid for and beautifully stylish like all the clothes he had insisted she should have.

'Why should you want to leave, *kyria*?' A gleam of insolence came into Aspasia's eyes, as if she knew all about the scene which had taken place in the *zala*. 'Don't you like being married to the *kyrios*?'

'That is none of your business——' Bliss broke off and made an effort to control her dislike of Aspasia, feeling a stab of revulsion that she must seek her assistance in leaving Paris. 'None of you, including Madame Apollonaris, want me to stay with him, and there's no danger involved where you're concerned. You work for his mother and he doesn't care to displease her.'

'His marriage to you has displeased her quite a lot.' Aspasia reached into a pocket of her robe and took from it a cigarette case and a lighter, and with her eyes intent upon Bliss she placed a cigarette between her lips, carried the flame to it and puffed smoke directly towards Bliss.

'You had a great argument with him, eh?'

Bliss refused to answer, and a knowing smile curled the woman's lips and more smoke was blown into the air. Suddenly Bliss couldn't endure the cheap smoke and the jibes, and she was on the point of thrusting Aspasia aside so she could go running back to her room when the woman took a threatening step forward.

'You argue with the *kyrios* like a child demanding all its own way, and you are fortunate that he stays his hand and doesn't teach you that the business of a wife is to please a man. You don't deserve him!'

'All you're fit for is listening at keyholes and spying on people,' Bliss rejoined. 'I'm getting out of here——'

'But I can arrange for a friend of mine to take you off the island, madame.' Aspasia drew deeply on her cigarette. 'Tomorrow, eh?'

'Early?' Bliss asked. 'Without my husband being aware?'

'My friend will do anything I ask of him—did you not see him on the caique when it brought you to Dovima?'

'He was one of the sailors?'

'*Ne*, madame.'

And it was something in the way Aspasia smiled that answered a troubling question for Bliss and she took an involuntary step backward.

'I see,' she exclaimed. 'So I'm hated that much by the *kyrios's* mother——'

'The *kyrios's* mother needed to say nothing to me about her feelings with regard to you.' Aspasia flung ash from her cigarette. 'I knew her feelings because I share them—as if a lily-skinned, sheltered little virgin like you could ever satisfy the desires of a man such as the *kyrios*! It is a nonsense! He has *zoikos*, that one! He is a man among men, and it would have been quick, over with, had that very same *zoikos* not sent him diving into the water to bring you out. Kristos tells me that you looked like a half-drowned cat, your wedding dress spoiled and your hair like seaweed!'

Suddenly Aspasia began to laugh, and Bliss felt a thrill of fear, a warning such as she had missed feeling on the *Stella Maris*, when a hand had hovered at her shoulder and thrust her over the rail into the sea while she had been bemused by the wedding wine and the bewildering ritual of becoming the wife of Paris Apollonaris. But now her thoughts were crystal clear, and they warned her that she must get out of this room as rapidly as possible.

Even as she frantically sought the door handle, Aspasia leapt at her and clutched her shining banner of silvery hair, jerking on it so that Bliss screamed with pain.

'Don't scream again.' Aspasia brought the cigarette's glowing tip to within a hair's breadth of Bliss's cheek. 'I would like to spoil your fine white skin for you, but it would look suspicious when you are found upon the rocks below the villa. Yes, *kyria*, my friend will certainly help you to get away from the *kyrios*, and it will be for good. There will be a sad funeral, and all who attend will say what a pity that the English girl fell over the cliffs on her honeymoon!'

Again Aspasia laughed, and Bliss felt another agonising jerk on her hair. 'You see, *kyria*, it will be remembered that on the caique you had a giddy fit and fell into the sea, and even the *kyrios* himself will not be suspicious.'

'Wh-what do you hope to gain?' Frightened as she was, and certain the woman was mad, Bliss had to keep her talking. Such people liked to talk about themselves.

'The *kyrios* will be a saddened widower and he will need to be consoled for his loss, and his mother is fond of me, you know. She would like it better if I were her daughter-in-law.' As

Aspasia spoke she eyed the stub of her cigarette, then put it to her lips to draw from it the last bit of comfort. 'The *kyrios* is a wealthy man, but after all he is not of the aristocracy, is he? His mother wants for nothing now, but she used to mind goats, so why should I not be good enough for him?'

'I'm sure you are,' Bliss said carefully. 'It was clever of you to pretend that you had only a little English. You really speak it quite well.'

'I know.' Aspasia smiled and slid her eyes over Bliss's face, strained by fear and the spiteful grip on her hair. 'You have no difficulty in understanding me, eh?'

Bliss could only pray madly that Paris would come looking for her so she could fling herself into the safe harbour of his arms and not let it matter that he had bought her as if she were an *objet d'art* he had seen displayed in a window that day he came to Cathlamet.

'I wished to learn English, and the *kyrios*'s mother arranged that I take lessons.' Once again Aspasia eyed the end of her cigarette and it was obvious that she needed to light another. 'Why shouldn't I be ambitious—I have good looks, and my hair is as fine as yours!'

'You wouldn't like it if I tried to pull your hair out by the roots,' Bliss murmured.

'No,' Aspasia agreed, 'but you don't count any more. You are going to be finished with.'

'If your friend took me across to the mainland, I promise you wouldn't hear of me again——'

'The *kyrios* would go after you and search for you.' With a nervous gesture Aspasia tossed aside the dead end of her cigarette, then awkwardly she reached across her own body in order to reach for another, which was in the case in the right-hand pocket of her robe. Bliss didn't hesitate; as she felt the slackening of the fingers in her hair she jerked backward and swung a blow across the bridge of Aspasia's nose.

This time it was Aspasia who screamed, a sound Bliss relished as she fled from that frightening room and yelled for Paris as she ran, crying the very house down for him.

To the end of her days Bliss would never forget the joyous lurch of her heart when she saw him bounding up the stairs towards her. Never forget the safe-keeping she felt when he caught her to him as if she were the most precious thing on God's good earth.

Doors were flung open and members of the staff milled about them, and disjointedly Bliss told of her experience with Aspasia. Grimly, then, she was handed over to the butler while Paris dealt with Aspasia.

The fearful sight of his rage wiped away for always any doubts in Bliss's heart that she wasn't loved by her husband. This time the tears that ran down her face were tears of relief, and she understood why a residue of Paris's anger was turned on her after the police departed in a launch, taking Aspasia and the sailor Kristos with them.

Paris prowled up and down the bedroom like a panther with a sore tooth, demanding to know why she would even think of running away from him.

'I never thought you would go that far,' he growled.

'Why not?' Curled up on the bed, the morning sun shining in her hair, Bliss looked at him with the wondering light of love in her clear grey eyes.

'Because,' he said fiercely, 'you know as well as I do that we belong together and that silly fights over bricks, slate and stone can never break us apart. When you ran towards me up there on that gallery you were running to your other half, and that is a fact! When I take you into my arms, *moiya*, I take you into my heart, and I hope to do so through day shine, through dark night, and through all the long years, if the gods grant us a long time together.'

'But you never said it,' she protested. 'I—I'm not a mind-reader, even if I did work for Madame Lilian.'

'You really will have to learn Greek.' Then he came to her, striding hungrily, picking her up as if she weighed no more than a child. 'When I hold you in my arms and speak to you of love, I do so in Greek—in Greek without thinking. Love you? Of course I love you! From the first moment I ever saw you, the sun in your lovely hair as it is right now.'

His arms tightened possessively about her. 'I employed your brother at my club in order to keep a link between us, not as you asserted because I wanted to make him steal from me. Because he was your brother, *pedhaki mou*, I believed him to be a better fellow than he was—will you now believe that I am a better man than you took me for?'

Bliss pressed her face against the side of his warm neck and pressed kisses to his skin.

'Paris,' she breathed, 'did you truly think that I'd walk out on you if you told me that Cathlamet had been burned down?' In the wake of the emotional storms it felt so good, this profound sense of peace that filled every crevice of her heart and mind.

'It wasn't a chance I was going to take,' he confessed. 'Nothing was going to stand in my way the day of our wedding—not a thing on this earth!'

'Not even your mother's disapproval of your English bride?'

'My mother will become reconciled, and you must never believe that she encouraged Aspasia to harm you.' Paris looked deeply into Bliss's eyes, as if he needed to dispel the last lingering shadow between them. 'My mother is a God-fearing woman, and she would not have stood in church with us had she harboured a real grudge against you.'

Bliss believed him . . . at last she believed entirely in the bliss they shared in each other's company. She gave herself to his kiss and the passion flowed warm and heady between them. There was no more sense of restraint and she could relish the fact that he was so adult, so fully aware of the fundamentals of life because he had never been blinded by love of brick, slate and stone.

'I love you,' he told her in English. 'But soon you will learn my language and you will understand me when I pour out my heart to you.

Always I shall feel my deepest feelings as a Greek, and it is my blessed wish that when we have a son he will have the lung power of his young mother.'

Bliss smiled, knowing that always they would share the memory of how she had fled into his arms, no longer the foolish girl who sought ghosts in the ruins of Cathlamet.

Paris was her strong and abiding haven.

Harlequin Photo Calendar

Turn Your Favorite Photo into a Calendar.

Uniquely yours, this 10x17½" calendar features your favorite photograph, with any name you wish in attractive lettering at the bottom. A delightfully personal and practical idea!

Send us your favorite color print, black-and-white print, negative, or slide, any size (we'll return it), along with **3** proofs of purchase (coupon below) from a June or July release of Harlequin Romance, Harlequin Presents, Harlequin Superromance, Harlequin American Romance or Harlequin Temptation, plus $5.75 (includes shipping and handling).

Harlequin Presents...

Take these 4 best-selling novels FREE

Yes! Four sophisticated, contemporary love stories by four world-famous authors of romance FREE, as your introduction to the Harlequin Presents subscription plan. Thrill to **Anne Mather**'s passionate story BORN OUT OF LOVE, set in the Caribbean.... Travel to darkest Africa in **Violet Winspear**'s TIME OF THE TEMPTRESS.... Let **Charlotte Lamb** take you to the fascinating world of London's Fleet Street in MAN'S WORLD .... Discover beautiful Greece in **Sally Wentworth**'s moving romance SAY HELLO TO YESTERDAY

Join the millions of avid Harlequin readers all over the world who delight in the magic of a really exciting novel. EIGHT great NEW titles published EACH MONTH! Each month you will get to know exciting, interesting, true-to-life people .... You'll be swept to distant lands you've dreamed of visiting .... Intrigue, adventure, romance, and the destiny of many lives will thrill you through each Harlequin Presents novel.

Harlequin Presents...

The very finest in romance fiction

Get all the latest books before they're sold out!

As a Harlequin subscriber you actually receive your personal copies of the latest Presents novels immediately after they come off the press, so you're sure of getting all 8 each month.

Cancel your subscription whenever you wish!

You don't have to buy any minimum number of books. Whenever you decide to stop your subscription just let us know and we'll cancel all further shipments.

Your FREE gift includes

Anne Mather—Born out of Love
Violet Winspear—Time of the Temptress
Charlotte Lamb—Man's World
Sally Wentworth—Say Hello to Yesterday

Exclusive Harlequin home subscriber benefits!

- SPECIAL LOW PRICES for home subscribers only
- CONVENIENCE of home delivery
- NO CHARGE for postage and handling
- FREE *Harlequin Romance Digest*®
- FREE BONUS books
- NEW TITLES 2 months ahead of retail
- MEMBER of the largest romance fiction book club in the world